JAMES STRAUSS

DOWN IN THE VALLEY

AN ARCH PATTON THRILLER

ISBN 978-1-540-7890-0-6

Contents

Also by James Strauss

The Boy
The Warrior
The Bering Sea

Visit www.JamesStraussAuthor.com for more!

I

How in hell he came to be lying in cloying dismal mud at the base of an extinct Hawaiian volcano eluded Arch. He just lay there, trying to catch his breath, knowing that the softness of the deep red earth was a death trap but not really having the energy to do much about it. He was sixty. Just days south of it. He didn't look sixty. That thought made him laugh, nearly aloud. If anyone were to see him in his current condition then looking sixty would be a major compliment.

The stream running right by him was clear and sparking bright. Arch diverted some of it with one hand, letting the water cascade over his upturned face, while he tried to rub what he could of himself clean with the other. Very gently he rolled out into the main current, the water running about six inches deep. He realized that his fall had not injured him badly. The soft mud had saved him, but it was nearly impossible to get it off once it attached itself to you. Red dirt, they called the stuff on Oahu. Some company even made clothing with the mud being used as a dye. "Awful red," Arch had called the pieces on display at a retail outlet across the island on Kalakaua Avenue.

He'd retired ten years ago before coming to be lying alone in the mud. Retired from being a field operations specialist. A real spy. A spy who had to get in and get out with almost no help, and accomplish missions which were too bizarre to be written into movie or television scripts. Spying wasn't a believable occupation. Not in the culture of modern America. So he portrayed himself as a retired professor, which he resembled much more than the public's idea of a spy.

He had nothing to show for his work. A small retirement from the Agency. A family, strewn across the landscape of his life, broken and dysfunctional. It didn't often bother him. But laying in the flowing stream, with cool mountain water washing over him for some reason caused him to think of his entire life and feel a deep sense of regret. In the words of some kid he'd overheard at an airport talking to another kid: "You have no life." Arch was left with no real life, and he knew it.

Agonizing a bit, he slowly sat up in the middle of the stream. The water was infusing him with life. He tried parts of his body. No broken bones. No cartilage not working, that he could tell. Only a feeling of immense fatigue. He'd been walking on the trail above only moments before, and now he was stuck in the stream at the bottom of a deep ravine.

"With not a friend in the world," he murmured to himself while twisting back to look upstream for the first time. What he saw surprised him to the point of working to breaking himself loose from the muddy bottom of the stream. With a long sucking sound, he pried himself out. A brown streak flowed downstream, as the water began to fill in the depression he vacated.

There was a body in the stream, not twenty yards from where Arch came to crouch, with his hands and knees still plunged into the wet red dirt of the bank. With deep rattling breaths coming from his lungs, he began to crawl on hands and knees, moving away from the bank again and out into the center of the gurgling water. There was no mud in the clear water coming down from the mountain, but the current worked against making rapid forward progress. It took him ten long minutes to reach the unmoving body.

Arch rose up to his feet, the water knee deep. He shakily gazed down at the prone form. A man lay before him on his back in the cocooning mud near the bank totally wrapped in gray duct tape. Even the man's eyes and mouth were taped over. The only way to tell that the body was of a male at all was by the lack of any swelling on its chest area. Arch couldn't judge if the body was alive or dead. He reached down with his right hand, dropping to one knee and went to work on one small corner of tape covering the body's mouth before pulling back sharply.

A plaintive croak came through the small hole the removal of the tape had allowed, and then some weak words.

"Help me," a male voice pleaded, the voice almost too raspy to understand.

Arch instantly recognized the voice. It had a distinctive nasal twang to it. Irritating. Just like the man it belonged to. Nathan Makaha Matisse. A man who'd almost written out his own death warrant by attempting to extort money from the United States Government for information that would have damaged that same government.

Moments earlier, in a clearing located somewhere above them, and following a very unsatisfactory conversation, Arch had told his associates to simply shoot the offensive idiot and leave his body in the brush for his relatives, or whomever, to find.

But here was Matisse, lying in the same stream bed as Arch, and begging for help.

Slowly, Arch peeled the tape from the man's eyes and ears.

"You're supposed to up there with a few bullet holes in you, so what are you doing down here?" Patton asked, tossing the small ball of used tape and watching it bob and float as it made its way downstream.

"Your friends thought it would be better to roll me down here to die slowly. Help me." Matisse struggled against the tape securing the rest of his body.

"Why should I help you?" Arch asked, trying to clean the red mud from his coated limbs. He noted that one of his Teva sandals was missing.

"Because you don't have a friend in this world. I'll be your friend," Matisse responded.

Arch stared at the man in surprise, and then was overcome by a fit of uncontrollable laughter. Finally, after more than half a minute he regained his aplomb.

" Just what makes you think that some lowlife scum like you, threatening the same government I've worked for so long and well, could ever be a friend of mine? I told those guys to shoot you," Arch finished.

"I forgive you," Matisse responded, "and besides, that was before we ended up in this mess. Why are you down here?"

Patton looked down at the wriggling creature before him, and then came to a decision. He began to pull the tape from the man's body one strip after another.

He said nothing until the sticky cloying operation was complete.

"I don't know what happened," he admitted to Matisse in a low voice, before pulling himself back up and out of the water. He waded over to sit on a nearby rock.

"You've got blood on the side of your head," Matisse said, pointing, as he struggled in the current to bring feeling back into his limbs.

Patton touched the spot Matisse had pointed at, and then jerked his head back in pain.

"Maybe your friends hit you over the head and dumped you down here with me," Matisse offered, wading through the shallow flow of water and settling atop a different rock not far away.

"Not bloody likely," Arch mused, more to himself than to Matisse. Patton's partner had stayed at the bottom of the trail, to await his return. A strike team of pro operatives had preceded him on-site to handle the rough work when Arch got to the location. They had all been strangers to him. But they were Agency operations people. There was absolutely no chance that a whole strike team, on American soil, was going to go rogue enough to do in a fellow agent, retired or otherwise. It just didn't happen that way no matter how Hollywood loved to portray it.

"Then what are you doing here?" Matisse wheedled, in his irritating nasal tone.

"What I'm doing here is why you're out of that tape, and likely to live. I don't know. Maybe I fell up there, hit my head, and rolled down the hill. I can't remember a damn thing."

"Not bloody likely," Matisse repeated Arch's words, trying to imitate his voice. He waited for a brief moment before inquiring further, "You'd remember falling at the very least. Do you?"

Arch thought about his last memory from above. He'd walked away to leave the wet work to the team. His job was done. He'd made the decision, and then given the orders. The last thing he recalled was beginning the return trip back down to where Frank, his partner, waited.

"No," Arch replied. "Something hit me on the head I guess, and then down I came."

"Ah, the cold blooded killer gets taken out." Matisse concluded, betting to his feet.

"Not in your case," Arch cut him off. "I told them to shoot you a few times, not kill you. Those are two different things. Bleeding, with a few holes added to your ugly local carcass, would have been convincing enough. I wouldn't have told you to leave that Bellow's thing alone if I was going to order you dead, if you recall."

Without further comment, both men moved and began working their way down the streambed, staying in the current to avoid becoming trapped in the mud that lined both sides of the moving water.

"Where we going?" Matisse asked, after awhile.

"Down in the valley. My partner's waiting with a car," Arch replied.

"Down in the valley, the valley so low, hang your head over, hear the wind blow..." sang Matisse, in a voice that was so deep and pure that Patton stopped in his tracks.

"What?" Matisse asked, stopping his performance. They stood looking at one another.

"That was beautiful. You have a great voice," Arch said, his tone one of complete surprise.

"Nah, all Hawaiians can sing. Haoles, like you, have no voice," Matisse responded.

They continued working their way down the valley together.

"Madonna's a Haole, and she can sing," Arch noted, after a few minutes.

"Life is a mystery," Matisse sang the beginning words to Madonna's song "Like a Prayer," but then stopped and went back to singing "Down in the Valley" while they waded on. Arch said nothing further until they reached an old concrete bridge running over the stream.

With Arch in the lead, both climbed the steep slope up to the road.

"What those Marines are doing in Sherwood Forest can't go on. People are going to die. My people," Matisse said, behind him.

"Sherwood Forest?" Patton asked, getting more of the red mud on himself as he climbed, and trying to shake it off while he went.

"Take from the rich, give to the poor. You call it Bellows Air Force Base." There's a lot of theft from all those tourist and military dependents vehicles going on there all the time.

"The poor being you local yokels and us Haoles being the rich, I suppose," Arch stated, his tone one of resignation. "And it's not your problem. That's a U.S. military base. They can do what they want there. It's U.S. government property."

"Radiation…. There is radiation coming from one of those canals, going right into our ocean," Matisse answered his voice low and filled with emotion.

Arch stopped climbing. "What are you talking about?" he asked.

"I took one of those Geiger counter things to the beach," Matisse responded. "Got it off eBay. Some of my friends turned red and got sick for a bit so I check out what the Internet said about stuff like that. Radiation made the Geiger counter sound like a chain saw. I know I can't stop the government from doing what they're doing. I just thought I could get some money because I know." Matisse stared into Arch's enlarged eyes when he stopped talking.

Arch sat down on the slope just down from the road. "Jesus Christ," he said, more to himself than the man he was with.

"You didn't know?" Matisse asked his voice one of surprise.

"No," Arch forced out. "I was raised on that beach. I camped there as an eagle scout when I was a kid. God damn it, there's no reason for anybody to have nuclear by-products there. The Marines use it for training, and that's all. Geiger counter or no Geiger counter I'm not sure I believe you."

"Why they build that fence on the inside of the road then?" Matisse asked. "And why they build a road inside that fence and patrol it with those M-Rap trucks?"

Arch rubbed his face, staying away from the painful part by his ear. The Marines had built a very well made security fence with wire at the top. He'd seen it himself. Local citizens were allowed inside Bellows to use the beach on weekends, but they could no longer park along most of the road. Huge rocks had been moved in to keep them from parking on the sand, as they had before. And what were the armored trucks there for, he wondered. And he'd seen the posted signs. The real high threat signs, that warned of the fatal harm that might be applied for trespassing. He had seen the same signs only once before in a place called Los Alamos, New Mexico. Those signs had been on the interior fences protecting nuclear tech areas.

"We take our kids there to swim," Matisse said, "and so do some of the Haoles who swim there."

"Still, there's just no way that there could be anything that would allow for radiation to be in the water. No way," Arch concluded, emphatically.

"Then what are you doing here? You come from mainland to see me? You bring those nasty people with you? To shoot me? How I become so famous? All that for me?" Matisse asked, before laughing.

Arch went back to climbing until he reached the top.

"No car. Frank's not there. Frank would not leave. Something's not right," he said, just as a man wielding a large branch broke from the nearby bracken. Arch ducked under the swinging chunk of wood, feeling compressed air whistle past his damaged head. He heard Matisse's yell behind him.

"No, Ahi, he's my friend. Don't hit him again," Matisse yelled.

"Again?" Arch asked up from his prone position on the ground.

"Ahi's my brother. He just protecting me," Matisse replied, taking Ahi's branch and heaving it back into the valley.

"Hello," Arch offered, making no move to shake the big Hawaiian's hand.

"Bro," the man responded, smiling a great white-toothed smile, as if hadn't just tried to take Arch's head off at the shoulders.

"I gotta car, but we have to go back over the ridge to get to it," Matisse said. "I parked up by the old abandoned reservoir. It's a Sunday car, only for me and my friends." He laughed lightly, as they walked, before going back to singing Down in the Valley. Ahi accompanied him in singing the song and walking with him side by side while Arch trailed both men wondering if he was not on the set of some alien horror movie made to resemble a bad sitcom.

"Why'd you come back to the island?" Matisse asked, when they broke from their duet.

"Back? How'd you know I was ever here before?" Arch answered.

"You Island Boy. Kamaina. You talk the pidgin when you not paying attention."

Arch frowned. He hated pidgin English. "Whasamattayou?" came instantly to his mind. Stupid talk from his childhood days in Waikiki.

"A woman," Arch finally stated, blurting out the truth as lying just didn't seem to matter under the circumstances. The Hawaiians said nothing, so he went on. "Her name's Virginia. I worked with her years back in South America, when were both fully active in the field. We had a bad go of it with some terrible people. They took out her ankle. Couldn't climb out and I saved her."

"Oh please," Matisse laughed and Ahi joined in. "You saved her and then you sleep with this Haole sista?"

Arch bit his lip. He hated that kind of talk. And he really hated that they had so quickly pegged his former relationship with Virginia. His one dalliance from his marital vows, even if the dalliance had been multiply performed across ten countries of the world. Virginia had not been the cause of his divorce. Poor selection in the beginning had been the cause, which his wife had proven by running off with another woman when the going got tough. Arch had not and could not ever come to terms with that part of his loss.

"Yes," Arch answered, not caring what the two locals knew. He'd come back for Virginia and she'd sent him on this seemingly simple errand. They'd planned the operation at the Officers Club on Kaneohe Marine Base so that was where he was bound. Virginia would have some understanding of what had happened. Virginia was as solid as rock but more beautiful and softer than any rock could hope to be. She remained single approaching fifty years in age. Arch liked to think that she'd been waiting for him over the past ten years of his agonizing and difficult divorce.

"You been set up, brudda," Matisse intoned. "And dat sista is the setup queen."

Patton crossed the top of the ridge behind the two locals. His breath came in pants, not from the difficulty of the climb but because of his roiling emotions. It simply wasn't possible. But why had Frank abandoned him? A partner, even a former partner never does that. If he hadn't, at least the car would have been there. Somewhere and for some reason orders had been handed down, guiding the mission into areas Arch hadn't been filled in on. Somehow he had become collateral damage on a mission he was supposed to be in charge of. But he hadn't been in charge of at all. He should have understood that from reflecting on his own retired status. A mission commander was always active and working real time in operations. A team leader was always in constant touch with some operational control, no matter how ancillary or distant.

Arch hadn't been in contact with anyone except Virginia and Frank, and that, following the planning phase, had been minimal....

II

Kaneohe Marine Base on the Windward Side of Oahu is among the best kept and most squared-away of all Marine bases. Nothing is out of place. Absolutely nothing out of place. Lawns are mowed with white rocks precisely set around their borders. Everything is so freshly painted that the Hawaiian trade winds are filled with the aroma. There is not one pothole on any of the streets. A civilian had once asked him how the Marines keep their bases so clean and tidy. Arch had just laughed. The man could not understand just how tight the discipline and work ethic of a Marine organization really was. There was no hired help. The Marines worked all the time when not training, eating or sleeping. It was simply part of being in the Corps.

"Stop here. I don't want you anywhere near the gate. Gimme your cell phone number and wait for my call. I've got to get to the bottom of this misunderstanding." Arch climbed from the back of the slowing Bonneville without opening the door. He jumped down just as the behemoth came to a halt. Matisse scribbled a number on a piece of paper and handed it to him.

"You got my six?" Matisse asked.

Arch locked eyes with the man. He reminded Arch of the character 'Angel' on Rockford, but even Angel had had some good traits. He nodded, and then turned to jog a half a mile to the Kaneohe main entrance.

At the gate, with no identification and in his disheveled state, it was little wonder the guards took him for some sort of interloper. He had to wait ten minutes for three Humvees to show up. That was no surprise. The cuffs and ankle chains were a shock, however. He said nothing, his anger overcoming every rational thought he could conjure up. They didn't even remove the Ghost of Christmas past ornaments when he was safely tucked into a concrete and steel cell. It took hours for Virginia to show up. Frank, his former 'partner' was with her.

They entered with two civilians wearing suits. Arch sat tucked in against the corner farthest from the stainless steel sink and toilet. He looked at the four impassively. The two civilians removed all the cuffs and chains, and then existed without comment, leaving the three of them alone.

"I suppose you want to know what this is all about?" Virginia began.

Arch stared for a moment before speaking. "Get him out of here. Whatever you are up to his conduct cannot and will not be forgiven or forgotten." No partner in a field operation ever abandoned his opposite number. That partner had to be the one person in the world who could be counted on. No matter what the mission Frank's conduct was unforgivable, and Arch intended that all of his acquaintances still with the Agency know about it.

Virginia nodded to Frank, who then turned and left, casting a contrite look over his shoulder as he went.

"Why'd you have me come to you? Did you think I wanted to run one last mission for the Gipper, or what? I came to Oahu because I've been in love with you for years, and you know it. I did this mission for you because of that. I've no idea of what you can possibly say about this or even why you are still standing in front of me in this cell?"

"We needed you to gain the trust of Matisse, Ahi and their movement."

Arch shook his head, the contusion on the side of it reminding him that he still needed some medical care.

"You were raised out here. You are both Haole and local. You can cross the cultural barriers. We can't recruit from his faction of the Sovereignty Sons Movement. Your treatment had to be convincing."

"To the point that I was knocked unconscious? With a contusion, double vision and the whole works that goes with Traumatic Brain Injury?" Arch muttered, his voice low but his tone scathing.

"This is a violent business, as you know. You've been a player for a long time and you know the risks, which were minimized in this case." She moved closer to where he sat. He could see mid-thigh up her skirt from his position on the floor. Even with what had happened and hating it Arch still felt her animal attraction. "We need you, and only you, just as I do." She knelt, cupped Arch's chin and kissed him full on the lips. Standing and backing away she extended one hand. A plastic card was held between her fingers.

Arch took the card and examined it. It was a hotel key to a room at the Turtle Bay Resort on the North Shore.

"We're done here. You have to decide. Room is two seventeen and I'll be there at seven tonight. You can go home or work with me on this. It's your call."

The door opened without her touching it and remained open. One of the civilian suits stepped inside, handed him a large grocery bag, and then departed leaving the steel door ajar.

Arch examined the contents of the bag. Polo shirt, Ralph Lauren shorts. Underpants, form fitting, and a set of Teva sandals were inside. Cash. About five hundred in twenties plus a Hawaii Driver's License, which he did not rate, and a military I.D. card. Everything was in his size and the data on the I.D.s correct. Inside the pocket of the shorts was a throwaway cell phone.

Arch stepped out of the cell. The civilian duo was stationed outside the door.

"Showers?" he asked.

They both pointed down the hall.

Shark's Cove on the North Shore near Sunset Beach has no sharks. Never did have any. Just a neat place of rough lave-reefed holes, just up from Waimea Bay. It's only for looking at when the winter waves crash onto the rocks. Any entry into such waters would be near instantly fatal. Arch, Matisse and Ahi sat on the edge of the park overlooking the scene. People scrubbed up nearby at the only fresh water shower publicly available for miles.

"Tell me," Arch said, breaking a silence punctuated only by breaking waves and the insistently hissing shower. "All of it. I'm the only thing keeping you alive. We can't be friends without candor. Just because I have your six doesn't mean we're friends. And if we become friends it'll probably only be because you don't have any others."

Matisse shifted uncomfortably. "You don't seem to be doing too great in that area either," he intoned. "Ahi, go look for sea shells on the beach." Matisse pointed to a lone twenty-foot square patch of sand a couple of hundred yards away. He waited several minutes while the big islander made his way toward the sand.

"We're taking Rabbit Island, off Bellows Beach. My people are digging in on the backside right now. We're bringing in water and plenty of food for a long stay. Succession is what we plan, until the United States accepts our terms. And if they want to play rough then we'll go public with the nuclear stuff or whatever it is."

Arch rubbed his face, and then his hair. He couldn't believe what he'd heard. "It's called Secession, not succession," he replied. "You're taking Rabbit Island? How the hell do you expect to hold it? You can't just occupy an island two miles offshore and stay there. It'll never be allowed."

"We got rifles. We got explosives. We got right on our side," Matisse answered waving his hands before him like he was directing a symphony. "What the police got? Small boats and some zodiacs. Won't last twenty minutes on the only small exposed beach there."

"Oh, I love this," Arch responded, laughing out loud. "Ah, I think you forgot about that little organization set up all over and behind Bellows. The United States Marine Corps, which has one simple mission in this world and it's called amphibious landing and assault."

"Nah, Brudda, da Marines are Federal. Rabbit Island is local. We got the comitatus working for us."

"I can't believe we might be friends. You are such an idiot. How can I save you from you? One phone call from the governor and you'll have a thousand Marines all over that island. And your rifles and explosives will be like cap guns and fire crackers. Posse comitatus only applies if the governor doesn't declare you a state of emergency. This friendship is going to be a very short one indeed."

Arch watched Ahi on the beach below, working at something in the sand. The huge man was crawling around on hands and knees looking for seashells. Arch felt like he was living a bad Sesame Street script. His partner and Virginia were not what or who they claimed to be, not in Arch's life, while his supposed new friends were completely ignorant idiots.

"They haven't a clue," Matisse pointed out, accentuating the phrase with one finger raised into the air. "Not one."

"Gee, you don't suppose they might be watching your idiot friends digging away on the backside of Rabbit Island with satellites, do you?"

Arch asked. "Virginia wants to know all about who everyone is. I'm surprised you're not in Gitmo tied to the bars and listening to acid rock. She's getting soft as she ages, but if she knows enough to tell me then she knows plenty about your operation on the island she didn't reveal."

Arch decided to mention nothing about his suspicions of Ahi. "Somebody's behind all this, driving this and it's not Virginia. Something big is going on or everyone wouldn't be acting so screwy. Get your buddy out of the sand and take me to Turtle Bay Resort. Come back tomorrow morning at six. And stay the hell away from everyone in your sovereignty outfit. You've got a mole. Your people on the island are armed. They're fair game. I said I'd watch your six. That's the best I can do."

It took fifteen minutes to get to the resort. Arch got out at the golf club parking lot a good distance from the front lobby doors. He didn't want anyone to know he was staying there. He hadn't even told Virginia when she'd slipped the room key to him that he was booked into the same hotel using a different identity. If she wanted to use all her power she might know anyway, but Arch was betting she didn't really care. The woman was mission focused with little room for personal considerations.

Arch stopped at the expansive front desk to check out the hotel floor plan. When he checked it out he smiled at his good fortune. He was on the fourth floor in a cheap South facing room. Virginia's room was directly across and two floors down facing east. Both rooms overlooked the tidal pool down below. Having stayed many times Arch had specifically asked for the cheaper view, as it was his favorite.

Arch took two hours to swim in the pool and lounge along the West shore of the resort. Waves, even though diminished in size for the summer, raged hypnotically close along the rocks on that side. Two Mai Tai drinks caused him no pain either. At six, he decided to call her room, using his cell.

She was in. Dinner would be at seven. Dinner would be at Ola, the beach restaurant where the chef was a wild man but a chef of the highest order. They would meet there supposedly for ease of parking, as Virginia remained under the impression he was coming in for the date. Arch dressed for the occasion. A lightweight Boss coat in dark blue, gray 120 trousers by Dunhill and an open Brioni white shirt. Sandals to soften and give a bit of island to the look. Coconut shampoo and conditioner by the resort. Hair brushed, not combed or gelled. He'd have preferred to simply toss on an Aloha shirt and keep the shorts but he knew Virginia would prefer more formal wear.

Arch stood on the edge of his small lanai waiting out the time and looking out as the sun began to set.

Hawaii was close to the equator. The sun arose around six and went down around seven without much variation at all. He glanced over at where he knew Virginia's room to be along the windows of the east wing, and was so surprised he instantly stepped back through his own open doors.

There were two men standing on her little lanai facing inward and obviously talking to someone inside. It was too far to identify them. By the time he unpacked his Leica binoculars the men were gone. It was disturbing, but no more. He was not totally sure he had the right room. And Virginia was in play. She was a busy woman and whatever the mission was she was working it. Arch was on a date. Virginia was making time for him. It was all he could expect. Or hope for, although deep inside his core still seethed with hurt and anger.

He left his room early, to avoid running into her in the main resort building. He took the long way around and arrived at the bar on the beach just outside Ola ten minutes early. Arch knew Virginia would be punctual to the second. It was one of her trademarks. Whatever the mission entailed it had already changed Arch's beliefs, relationships and quite possibly his life.

III

rch completely understood Virginia's need to toss him from the room and get on her cell phone. The active career he'd only recently retired from demanded he understand and leave immediately after the short dinner and even shorter get together in her room. The mess of her room that they'd destroyed together seemed such a warm and inviting relief from the rest of Arch's mostly cold universe.

"Might go over to Ola's for a nightcap," Arch said back to her, as she closed the door, cell phone already glued to one ear. He went up to his room to clean up and call it a night, although it was only nine o'clock. They hadn't talked about he mission or what had happened to him during dinner or after. It was like either there was no real mission or they had been allowed a recess for personal time. He went back to his room to freshen up and change shirts, but couldn't help checking out Virginia's lanai one more time before he went.

Number 217 was brightly lit, Arch noted, but that wasn't what drew him to peer out from inside his own darkened room with the Leica fifty millimeters. The two men had returned to her small outside lanai, standing as before, facing inward. The Leica's brought both into sharp relief. Arch had never seen either man before. They wore casual trousers and aloha shirts. One man wore loafers while the other gave himself away by wearing hand-worked spit-shined shoes common only to elite elements of the military. He also wore white socks. Arch kept a pair of shoes just like them, always ready in little cloth bags at the front of his closet in Santa Fe, but would have rather been caught dead than wearing them with shorts and white socks. Virginia was back practicing her craft.

He focused the Leica binoculars on Ola Bar and Grill located just above the sand beyond the tidal pool area. There were few people around, although the place would remain open until midnight. Flambeau, the crazy chef, could be seen moving quickly about, wearing his bright white and spotless cotton coat. Arch smiled. He liked the expressive man. He decided to spend the rest of his waking hours at the bar, regardless of what Virginia decided. Being entertained by the chef's outrageous cooking stories would be fun, no matter what, and his cooking was some of the best on the island.

Arch tossed the glasses on his bed and headed out.

There were only two ways to get to Ola from the main building. Both ways came together at the apex of a "Y" just before the restaurant entrance; the nexus of the "Y" was in the middle of a dark overhanging cluster of tree branches and dense tropical bushes. It was there they took him.

Some sort of heavy padded object struck Arch on the side of his head, stunning him to the point of collapse, although he never impacted onto the crushed coral lining the path. Strong arms grabbed and carried him away. The only thought that rose to the top of his semi-conscious mind was relief. He hadn't been struck on the side of his head with the healing contusion he'd received from the earlier tree branch. His wrists and eyes were taped in seconds, as the men held him pinned against the side of big black rental car.

Instantly, he was hoisted into the air and plopped uncomfortably atop the spare tire in the car's trunk. Arch tried to think through the pain and mark the vehicle's passage as it pulled away.

He could feel the rental pass over the speed bumps built into the private road leading out of the resort. The car turned right onto Kam Highway. Arch began to count. He knew the team members who had him were pros. They were too fast and too well coordinated to be anything else. And no crew of robbers was dumb enough to penetrate deep into the body of a huge resort and simply cart away one man in the dark. The car would not speed to avoid police interference. The limit was forty-five on Kam Highway, which took about seventy seconds per mile. The Lincoln, or whatever full size car it was, turned after three hundred seconds, or about four miles by Arch's count. He knew the area. They'd had to pass through one signal in front of the only grocery store on the North shore but it must have been green, as they hadn't stopped. They were moving a short distance toward the ocean just before Sunset Beach. There was only a short distance they could move before they'd be in the water. He tried to remember what was located along that part of the shore, other than super-expensive luxury homes. The car came to an abrupt stop.

The trunk popped and Arch was painfully pulled from the floor. He gave no resistance, simply trying to prevent more bruising by being banged about in his blind condition. He walked, guided by two men holding his elbows. Nobody talked. The men opened a door, took him through, flipped him around and sat him in some sort of wooden chair. He could hear the duct tape being stripped from a roll before it was used to tape his wrists to long flat handles protruding out from under them. Arch concluded that the chair was an outdoor Adirondack sort of thing.

"Sit there and shut up. Somebody wants to have a word with you," a deep raspy voice stated flatly. The door slammed and the men were gone.

Arch wondered if the room was lit. They'd taped his right wrist bare, with the tape covering his skin, but his left wrist was taped over the cuff of the long sleeve shirt he'd chosen to ward off the cool trade winds from the ocean that swept through Ola's open windows during evening hours. He could twist, turn and lever the wrist. He concluded, with his eyes still covered, that the room had to be dark or the men would never have made that mistake.

After only a few moments Arch was able to gently pull his left hand through the sleeve of his shirt, but he didn't try to fully break free. He calculated that there were at least four men outside the closed door. Arch knew he was no match for them. He didn't even know if they were armed, but had to assume so. He had to have more information about the shack he was in. He knew it was one of the few surfer shacks left on the expensive pristine shore. Why there were any left at all Arch never understood. Inexplicably some had survived the ravages of constant salt spray and onset of rapid development around them. Instead of trying to pull free from the chair Arch leaned forward so his face was close to his left hand, which he could move fairly easily. He worked the blinding tape over his eyes loose until he felt a small space break free between the tape and his left cheek. He needed some vision, although he could see nothing in the total darkness.

Arch sat with his back pressed against the hard wood of the severely angled Adirondack. He thought about what had taken place on the mission, which was not supposed to be a mission, until he'd come to arrive in the chair. He hadn't been truly angry before but he was rapidly becoming so. Possibly, he'd passed on his only chance to break free by not taking advantage of the amateur taping job of his captors. He realized that but no longer care. He'd become enraged to the point of not caring. In all of his years as a successful field agent he'd never been in such a personally compromising situation. That he was, and that it seemed at the hands of his own people, was humiliating and more than enraging. The door opened. A sliver of light penetrated through the crack at the bottom of his left eye. Arch could make out the clapboard floor of the shack.

"Hello," a friendly male voice said from a position just to his right side. The tone caused a small shiver of fear to run up and down Arch's back. Aggressiveness was an understood quality in the business he'd been in. Calm delivery, such as what he was hearing, was the sign of a very serious, professional, and quite probably at least a mildly sociopathic player. Arch didn't reply.

"We have some questions. And we need some immediate answers. I'm not going to ask any questions just yet. I need you to understand how serious we are."

A lancing bright pain caused Arch to flinch as a needle was punched into his thigh, right through his light twill trousers.

"You're going to grow quite violently ill for about fifteen minutes. I'll return and give you another shot that'll make you feel okay again. We have all night to go through this however many times you feel comfortable with." The door opened and closed. The light went out. And then the nausea hit.

Waves of sickness swept through him, like ever increasing ocean waves in a set, but the set never stopped. Projectile vomiting every ten seconds fouled his pants and shoes as he leaned as far forward as he could to keep from choking on vomit, until there was no more vomit. And then the sickness got worse. His stomach heaved into spasms that he could not stop. The pain of the spasms was almost too much to bear. Arch went back to Vietnam. The shots that had pierced his torso had caused the same pain. He'd withstood that pain without medication for five hours by controlling only those things he could. He slowed his breathing between the waves of pain. He imagined his heart and worked to slow that, while also thinking about and working on his blood pressure. An age later the door opened and lights were again thrown on. Another sharp pain, this time in his right shoulder, brought Arch out of his concentration. He gasped. The door closed, but this time the light remained. The nausea began to fade. The speed of its departure induced euphoria, as the sickness and pain passed to the point where it seemed, except for the wetness and stink of his vomit, as if it'd never occurred at all.

The door opened and closed again. "Hello," came from the player standing in front of him, although far enough away to be outside the radius of the mess Arch had made. "I do so hope you are going to go along with me on this."

"Okay," Arch rasped out. Whatever the men wanted to know simply was not worth the suffering. Torture, physical torture, always worked Arch knew from his long experience. At some point of applying terrible the subject always came to decision point. The worth of the information requested, when weighed against the ever-increasing terror and pain, overwhelmed the decision-making process. Arch had been shot, whipped, poisoned and knifed, but he'd never been deliberately restrained and tortured before. His understanding of surrendering in the face of real visceral experience was new although his decision was analytical. He just didn't give a damn about the mission, the Agency or even Virginia anymore.

"Oh good. I do so hate the detestable mess we end up with using this process. Blood is easier to bear, but I do have the instructions I must follow. I'm sure you understand," the man finished and waited. His tone and the way in which he expressed himself scared Arch even through his rage. For the first time he wondered if he was going to survive the questioning. The only hopeful note in the man's delivery had been about his having 'instructions.' The fact that blood had apparently been ruled out seemed to weigh in Arch's favor, but he was anything but certain.

"Exactly what do those crazy Hawaiians have in weaponry and pyrotechnics on Manana Island?" the man asked.

Arch knew the man was talking about Rabbit Island. Manana was the formal name for the place, located just off of Bellows Beach and known to so many Americans simply because it was in almost every backdrop of Robin's Nest in the T.V. show *Magnum P.I.* The locals had renamed the place many years. Rabbits had been raised there for butchering at one time in the distant past, hence the name. Tourists thought the island was named rabbit because it looked like a laying rabbit, which amazingly, it did.

Arch blabbed everything he knew about what Matisse had told him, even adding some grenades and rockets to make it sound the more believable.

"Good, good, you're doing fine," the smarmy dangerous player intoned, as if he was encouraging some fourth grader to snitch on his companions.

"About this nuclear detection stuff, crazy as it seems. Do they have a scintillation counter over there, or has one been used?"

Arch began a long uncontrolled inhalation of his breath. He focused the lens of his left eye to peer beyond his spray of vomit to the feet of the man before him. Brightly shined shoes with white socks. A glint of light sparkled off the man's regulation shoes. Scintillation. The word last used only hours before by Virginia, now repeated by one of the men who'd stood talking back to her on the lanai of Room 217.

"I've never heard of a scintillation counter and I don't think they have either," he replied, truthfully. "These locals aren't technologically savvy at all. I think Matisse has an old WWII surplus Geiger counter, but that's it. I don't think it's very accurate either, as I passed it over my watch hands and it went crazy," Arch lied. He had no idea where or what Matisse's Geiger counter was and his Breguet chronometer used Lumi-Nova hands, not the old radium things that'd been radioactive.

"Stay here," the spit-shined shoe man said, using more of his strange stupid humor. "I must consult with my associates."

Arch worked his left hand back out of his sleeve under the tape, but his timing proved terrible. The door opened and a man wearing loafers appeared and grabbed Arch's arm before he could do anything.

"Ah, our prisoner thinks he's leaving, eh? Not just yet he's not. I've been waiting to use this for a long time on some asshole like you," the man's deep voiced whisper penetrated to Arch's very soul. His imagination ran wild with whatever device the man could be talking about. Suddenly, the deadly evil of the shoe-shined man was preferable to what was in front of him.

The man worked with something he'd taken from a shelf nearby. Soft metal on metal sounds permeated the inside of the shack, and then the movement of a metallic action. Arch heard two hard but quiet 'swishes' before cold metal pressed down hard on his left hand to the flat wooden chair handle. Three louder bangs cause Arch to grunt and curl himself inward in extreme pain. He would have screamed but nothing would come out except a pitiful mewling sound.

"What was that," the soft-sounding sounding player asked, obviously from just outside the door.

"I just nailed this Haole to his chair. He was trying to escape. I love this God damned automatic nailer thing," the raspy man replied. The sound of three more bangs in quick succession took place, with resulting impacts against one of the wooden walls nearby.

"Put that thing down. No blood. Our instructions were clear. Are you a complete idiot?"

"No blood," the raspy-voiced man replied. "Look. Clean as a whistle. He'll be some time getting out of that chair."

"Jesus Christ. Take that thing out of here. Leave him. We're done here," the shoe-shined man instructed. After a few minutes of what sounded like preparations to leave the man leaned back through the door. "Sorry about him. I'm sure you'll be fine. Just needed some data. Sure you can understand."

Arch listened to the men depart. The door was left gaping open with the light on. Arch's left hand was aflame in pain. Through the crack under the tape he could see the heads of three nails, neatly appearing in a row behind the knuckles and between the bones on the surface of his splayed out left hand. The nailing man had not lied. There was no blood at all. But the man had made a mistake. The great force of the driven nails had split the vertical arm support into several failing pieces. Arch breathed in and out, gathering his strength and endurance. The pain in his head, and the pain from the sickening shot, and even the pain of the nails sticking through his hand were nothing to pain in his heart.

"Virginia," he screamed in whisper, in agony of body and mind. Arch tore the handle from the chair, blood flowing amongst the other fluids he'd expelled.

IV

rch fought the chair, sounds of pain emanating from deep down in his chest. His left arm finally came loose but a three-foot section of wood remained attached to his hand by the hard driven nails. There would be no release from the wood or the pain until he got some kind help or proper tools. It took almost half an hour to work his other hand out of the duct tape. With that raw sticky hand he was able to peel the covering from his eyes. He wondered if he would have any eyebrows or lashes when he again looked at himself in a mirror.

There was nothing usable in the shack. He stepped outside and took three darkened steps down to the beach, where gentle surf broke twenty yards further out in the night. The moon was almost full. Arch could make out a white line of surf, which extended for miles east along the curve of the elongated cove. He'd already decided not to go to the authorities. The mission had become the most personal of his life and he was going to keep it that way if at all possible.

Even cradling the long chunk of wood with his good hand, moving through the deep sand caused him agonizing pain with every step. His head throbbed where he'd been sandbagged and his older contusion was inflamed by the spray from nearby breaking waves. Arch tried to walk between the surf and the dry sand, as the surface was harder, but the going was slow. There were three coves between the shack and the Turtle Bay resort. When it finally came into view, less than half mile away, he made a decision to stop. He had no idea what lay waiting there. Matisse would be along in his Sunday car to pick him up at six if he was lucky. Arch checked the Breguet. It was one in the morning. He huddled down in the warm sand, as far from the sea as he could get without being fully into the brush and trees beyond. He curled into a fetal ball, expecting to remain awake until near dawn, but in spite of the throbbing pain he was asleep in seconds.

It was five when he awoke. He rolled over, forgetting about his pinned hand, and let out a stifled scream. In the pre-dawn light he could see that the hand was swollen to twice its normal size. The pain was even worse than before. Fighting tears Arch staggered into the trees, working east, going from one slanting horse path to another. The resort offered horse rides but nobody would be active before nine. By the time he could see the access road leading to the unmanned security gate into the resort he could also see the outlandish, but welcome, Pontiac. Matisse had pulled off Kam Highway to wait, somehow figuring that Arch would come out to him.

"Brah, you look like shit. What happened?" Matisse asked, opening the rear door to help Arch crawl onto the seat. "You got chunk a wood stuck to your arm and your head looks like a Kahuku melon. We go hospital."

"No," Arch countered. "We need some tools to get my hand loose. And I need a gun. Do you have a gun?" Arch laid flat atop the lengthy bench of the old Pontiac's cavernous back seat. The wood attached to his hand rested across a raised hump containing the car's drivetrain.

"I got two guns," Matisse answered, "both registered so I don't get no trouble. I take you home. How you get the wood stucka your hand?"

Arch sighed with his eyes closed, as wind began to blow over the edges of the open convertible. Matisse was afraid of gun registration trouble while he was attempting to lead his movement in seceding from the United States of America. He would have laughed if he hadn't been in so much agony. For once he didn't care that Matisse was racing along the precarious two-lane highway at well over the speed limit.

Somewhere along the Haleiwa cutoff Matisse turned the car onto a dirt side road.

Arch watched overhanging cane and coconut palms fly by above him for several minutes until the Pontiac skidded to a stop.

"I get the tools. We need big pliers, maybe a saw and a hammer. I don't know, but I get 'em. My wife Gail here to help." Matisse's head disappeared from Arch's view to be replaced by an angelically beautiful face.

"Gail Kalauokalani," the angelic woman said. "You don't look good at all. Can you get up?"

Arch knew he would not be able to pronounce the last name without practicing but he could handle the first. "Yeah, I can, and thank you Gail," he answered, slowly rising up to sit in the back seat. A single ply stilt house sat not far away. Once it had been white but everything Arch looked at in and around the place was the same color. An awful brownish stained color of dried lava mud.

Matisse returned with a paper grocery sack full of tools. With an unwilling groan Arch moved to the driver's side of the vehicle and raised his arm and the wood to rest upon the top edge of the back door. Matisse went to work with two over-size pliers, twisting and breaking off bits of wood. Every move caused Arch agony, but he worked to control himself. Gail returned with a kitchen towel filled with ice cubes. She gently eased it to the freshly damaged side of his head, and then patiently held it there. After ten minutes Matisse let out a celebratory exclamation.

"Cowabunga!" he yelled. "I got da sucker off. Now we got da nails to deal with."

Arch peered down at his hand. Three nails at least four inches in length stuck between the fingers of his left hand. He could move the swollen fingers so he figured no bones were broken, but he had little feeling other than pain. Nerve damage might be a future problem.

Matisse turned the damaged hand so the palm faced up. He took out his hammer.

"No way to do this nice. Sorry Brudda," Matisse said, and then struck one of the nails on its point.

The pain was excruciating. Arch jerked, unable to stop himself, and cried out. Regaining control he stared at the offending nail. It had been driven half way out.

Matisse repeated the process for the remaining nails, and then used his pliers to extract them completely. Arch almost passed out several times, only saved by the ice pack held to the side of his head and the Gail's gently massaging hands.

Matisse cut strips from a second washcloth to make bandages. "Man, you gotta get a Tetanus shot for that stuff. Why would someone nail your hand to a chunk of wood? You got some real crazy friends."

"Guns," Arch stated, flatly. "You said you had guns. Get them, please."

Gail stepped back upon hearing Arch's request. She took his good hand and showed him how to support the ice pack, then turned to follow her husband into the stilted house. Arch heard muffled arguing inside, but after a few minutes Matisse came out carrying a broken down cardboard shoebox. He set it on the seat beside Arch.

"My wife's worried. She thinks you might get me into big trouble. I told her not to worry. You have good judgment for a Haole. She doesn't know about Rabbit Island or any of that."

"No kidding," Arch said, clutching his bandaged hand to his stomach. He put the ice pack down and took the top off the shoebox with his good hand. Two guns, just as Matisse said, both covered in a single oily cloth. Arch unwrapped them. A Smith and Wesson four inch forty-four magnum. A fearsome hand weapon. It was empty, as was the forty-five Colt that accompanied it. The Colt was one of the older Mark IV models made of real steel, not the weaker alloys used later on. Six boxes of ammo were wedged into the container with the weapons. One box of ball for the forty-five and two of hollow points. The magnum rounds were all hollow points except for half a box of shot shells. Arch examined the curious shot shells before loading both weapons. Two bird shot shells for the .44 and four hollow points. Two ball atop the .45 magazine and five hollow points further down.

"What you gonna do, brah?" Matisse asked him.

"Visit some interesting folks back at the resort," Arch answered him, truthfully. "I need to borrow your car."

"No way," Matisse responded. You not drive like that. Not my Bonneville. You look like Kilauea Volcano just after erupting. I drive. I'm your friend now. I make this visit with you."

Arch groaned. Matisse was not a player. He was a troubled and troublesome citizen. There was almost no doubt at all that the Hawaiian's guns had never been fired at all, much less in anger or for any kind of operational mission. The man was a liability where Arch was going, but he had little choice. Arch's eyes, stability, hand and head were a mess, and his psychology was bent at least ten degrees from top dead center he knew, as well.

"Back to Turtle Bay," Arch agreed, pointing his good hand east.

Arch had Matisse drive right up to the security gate, which was manned for unknown reasons.

"William Farrell, I'm a guest," he told the woman at the gate, as the unlikely big Pontiac idled in front of the button controlled wooden bar in front of it.

The woman checked her computer. "Got some I.D.?" she asked.

Arch produced a California driver's license, glad his 'questioners' had not taken any of his personal items. He carried three of his old identities at all times. Each identity came back to the same set of prints. The police had run his prints only once since he'd retired. Somehow one of the driver's licenses had been suspended without his knowledge. It had taken hours before the local cops released him. Thy tried but never solved the mystery of how three identities could come back to the same set of prints.

As they drove to the upper resort parking lot, Matisse asked questions. "Will Farrell? Isn't he an actor, or something? Like a movie actor? Or television? Arch didn't answer, as he didn't feel like explaining his own sense of humor about identities that he'd picked up from Chevy Chase's role in the movie Fletch. After a moment of silence Matisse went on to his next question. "What you want me to do here?"

"Wait in the car. I'm going to Virginia's room to get to the bottom of this mess. Either something major is going on or this is one of those ridiculous and idiotic dog and pony shows that happen every once and awhile in the business. I can't imagine anything like that happening with Virginia involved though.

It was a short walk to the lobby. Arch had dumped the .45 under the rug of the Bonneville's back floor, along with the extra ammunition. He carried a pocketful of shot shells and hollow points for the magnum. The gun itself was in its shoebox. Innocuous enough. It was almost eight o'clock in the morning. Maids were already working the wing that Room 217 was in. His luck was good. The door to 215 was propped open with a maid's cart just outside. A short Filipino woman moved from the room to her cart.

Arch backed behind the elevators and looked over to where the ice machine stood.

Carefully and laboriously, with one arm and shoulder he eased it away from the wall, and then pulled the plug. He shoved it back in with his back as best he could.

When he got to the maid's cart he removed an extra plastic ice bucket from the backside. He waited for the woman to come from the room.

"The ice machine is broken," Arch said, holding out the ice bucket in his good hand. Could you get me a bucket of ice?" Arch asked, as the woman continued unloading some supplies from her cart. He produced a twenty when she accepted the bucket into her hand. "For housekeeping," he smiled, hoping she wouldn't notice his swollen head or the damaged hand clutching an old shoebox.

The woman's eyes were glued to the twenty. She accepted it, looking down the hall once before slipping it into a small pocket of her apron. As he hoped, she left the room door to 215 propped open.

Moving quickly, once the maid disappeared on her way to the service elevators all the way at the end of another wing, Arch pulled the gun from the shoebox, stuck the box in the maid's trash bag, and eased quietly and carefully to the sliding glass window. He jammed the short but bulky weapon into his right front pocket. Once on the small lanai he stared over at the lanai to 217, Virginia's room. The railings to the two rooms were within a couple of feet of one another, which would have been no problem if Arch weren't so injured. Arch looked down. It was about twenty-five feet to the roof of the lobby. If he fell he wouldn't be walking again for months, if ever.

Using his good right hand Arch gripped the horizontal top rail and stared at the two-foot space separating the lanais. He brought his left leg up and over the rail and then his right. Balancing on his butt, and leaning into his grasping right hand, he moved to insert his feet between the opposite bar railings. Once positioned with his butt on one railing and his feet between the rails of the other he heaved his upper body forward and plummeted over the railing in front of him and onto the floor of 217's lanai, wondering if the thudding sound his body made would wake Virginia. If she was asleep. If she was even there. The move succeeded and the sound of his body hitting the floor was only slight compared to the muffled scream that was forced from his throat when his damaged hand hit the opposite railing.

The window was fully open but the drapes were closed and billowing outwards, disturbed by early morning trade winds. Arch got control of himself and then peered into the darkened room. There was no sign of Virginia, but the two men who'd once stood on her lanai talking, and then ended up in the surfer's shack with him, were asleep side by side on their backs atop the king size bed. Neither of them had apparently been disturbed from sleep by the noise of Arch's landing.

"Screw it," Arch whispered to himself inaudibly, and then entered the room. As quietly as possible, and without turning, he closed the sliding glass window behind him. It took several minutes because of the blowing drapes and Arch's inability to touch or manipulate anything with his damaged hand. Once the slicing door was closed, with the drapes unmoving and drawn, the room was in near total darkness. Arch had memorized the placement of every object in the room, however. Without any hesitation he moved to the bed, grabbed one of the extra pillows discarded to the floor and removed the Magnum from his pocket. With his bandaged hand, his pain somehow held in abeyance, he placed the pillow over the raspy-voiced man's extended right hand. Jamming the short barrel of the .44 into the pillow he pulled the double action trigger.

The sound was similar to that of striking a wooden desk hard with a baseball bat. The sound of the gun was changed to something else. A very loud sound but not identifiable as a gunshot. The man screamed in anguish. Arch turned on the sidelight, his revolver aimed directly at the head of the second man, the one who'd worn the spit-shine shoes. The man didn't move or make a sound, although his unblinking eyes grew round as he recognized the intruder.

"Shut up," Arch hissed at the injured man, pressing the holed pillow down hard on his shattered hand. The man continued to cry softly, clutching the pillow and his hand to him, but there was no more screaming.

"There were some questions you forgot to ask. So I came back to help. Surely you can understand," Arch said, staring deeply into the very dangerous man's eyes.

V

W hat do you want?" the formerly dangerous man on the bed said, his voice im-
ploring, extending his arms out before
him with both palms turned upward in question.

"You forgot to ask a few questions you needed the
answers to. Answers that would have avoided this very
meeting. I thought Virginia was smarter but it appears
fairly obvious she left a few things out." Arch said the
words without emotion, standing well back from the
bed so both subdued men could be kept sufficiently far
from the steady end of the magnum's short but cavernous barrel.

"I worked for the Agency for twenty years, performing various mission in wet work," Arch went on.
"I'm responsible for the departure of 37 targets, not
including collateral damage from area weapons. There
was no chance on God's green earth that you would be
able to handle somebody like me without killing me.
So here you are, waiting for me to decide what to do
with you. What should we do with you, by the way?"

"Shit," the man with his palms upraised said very softly, slowly lowering his hands. "We're dead men? Over something like this?"

"Dead?" the wounded man mewled out, clutching his bloody hand with the punctured pillow. "Dead? You're going to kill us?"

"Idiots," Arch spat out in disgust. "Total idiot knuckle-draggers. Where in hell do they find you people? I can't kill you. You're with the Agency. I'd love to kill you. Cook you slowly for days over a charcoal spit. I can, however, maim you for the rest of your lives. So, given that prospect, what in hell was this all about?" Arch held up his own injured hand. The man laying on the bed carefully shook his head, and then looked over at his wounded companion.

"It wasn't Ms. Westray's idea," the man on the bed said. "The general thought you might need some motivation to give us the information. My name's Lorrie, and this is Kurt," the man pointed at his bloody companion.

"What general?" Arch asked, mystified, and also wondering why the man hadn't used Virginia's first name. Last names were sometimes used in fieldwork but almost never with any kind of honorific.

"The Marine general at the base. The one running this whole thing. Dewar. The one star."

"Brigadier Dewar? The Brigade Commander at Kaneohe?" Arch lowered the magnum. A Marine general. It made sense. The strange goings on over at Bellows with radiation. The totally screwed up mission with agents working against one another instead of together. The whole thing stunk of military involvement leading to misunderstanding and violent failure. The famous President Carter mission to save the hostages in Iran came to Arch's mind.

"The woman's real close to the general but he doesn't tell her everything," Lorrie said, beginning to visibly relax for the first time.

"Real close?" Arch asked, putting the magnum back in his pocket. He couldn't even maim the men for what they'd done. They simply didn't know any better.

"Yeah, they're an item. He's married but his wife has no clue. She doesn't seem to care. I heard her tell him she preferred married men. No obligations."

Arch wanted to sit down. His mind had been a hot bed of angst and anger, thinking Virginia had turned him over to torturers without a second thought. But the news from Lorrie was even worse. He looked closely at the man for any hint of deception. He couldn't pick up a thing. He was almost certain neither man knew of his previous intimate visit with Virginia. What motive would the man have to lie? His relief at not being hurt further or killed was just too evident.

"Get your little package of DZ sick crap out," Arch ordered harshly, in an attempt to bring his mind back into some kind of mission orientation.

"Look, I used that to be humane. Please don't give any of it to me," Laurie begged while gently easing a little black leather case from inside his left front pocket.

"Please? That's the best you can do, after using it on me?" Arch grimaced, taking the case from Lorrie's hand. He put it into one of his own pockets. "I've no intention of using it on you. Do you suppose the general had some other reason for sending you guys?" Arch's mind ran to its darkest depths as he considered the situation. Was the general having an affair with Virginia? Everything pointed to it. Had Virginia come to bed with Arch straight from the general's bed? Unanswerable questions rolled through Arch's mind, like waves coming at the beach in a never-ending set. One thing was for certain; Arch wasn't going to get anything of real use out of the two minor players in front of him.

"Get him to the base," Arch said, pointing at the man with his bleeding hand. "Any civilian ER will have you both taken in custody, where you belong, but we can't have that, now can we?" Arch laughed but the sound rang hollow in the room, even to Arch's own ears. "Get out quickly. Using that pillow for a suppressor probably didn't fool too many people and security in this place will probably be along anytime."

"Thanks," Lorrie answered with obvious relief, working to get his partner Kurt vertical and off the bed.

"Think nothing of it," Arch replied, his voice laced with acid. "When you see Virginia tell her that I've gone rogue, and I'm damn sure going to put a huge monkey wrench into all of their plans. And please report to the general that certain body parts of his are going to look like what's left of Kurt's hand when I'm done." Arch was disappointed in himself as soon as the words were out. He was getting old. Predators in the business, players, never threatened. They simply did. If anything they sent waves of kindness, respect and even love before them, before they killed the intended prey.

Arch made it to the elevators unimpeded. The maid's cart was still in front of 215 with the door propped open, but there was nobody to be seen.

Once inside his own room Arch went to his laptop and started to work. It took seconds to discover that a scintillation detector a device was used to measure how much irradiated iodine was present in a sample. A regular Geiger counter was not sensitive enough to measure dosages so low as to cause cancer-producing radiation in iodine. Irradiated iodine isotopes are the first and most damaging elements to be released from a spill of nuclear fission material. Most fissionable metals are comprised of up to three percent iodine. A good dosage of irradiated iodine would cause thyroid cancer in only a few years, to anyone so exposed.

Arch sat back in his chair. He thought about the events he'd just been through. Scintillation had been mentioned by Virginia and Lorrie both. Scintillation was not a common word for any intelligence agent to know about or understand. Lorrie was lying about some of what he said. Was he lying about the general and Virginia? And what in hell was going on at Bellows? No wonder the Marines were spooked by Matisse and his unlikely band of sovereignty idiots. The poorly timed venture of the islanders, parking themselves on an island right in the middle of whatever was happening, must have been shocking to the players running whatever show they were running. Arch laughed out loud, imagining Matisse running around nearby holding out a Geiger counter.

He headed out to join Matisse. It was time to encounter Bellows Air Force Base up close and in person. Arch had trained there while attending his last two years of military school. Bellows, in the fifties, following its deactivation as an actual flight base for the military, had served as the Oahu home for the Civil Air Patrol. Arch had soloed there in a glider before being dumped from the program for crashing three gliders and being dumped for insubordination behavior directed at the group commander. Arch remembered the base well, and also the fact that there was a nearby peak off base that he'd used to circle and gain altitude in his glider training days. From the top of that peak, just below the huge menacing Koolau range, every part of Bellows could be viewed with high definition binoculars. The Leica binoculars might, once again, prove invaluable.

Matisse was waiting, just as before, when Arch completed his hike out from the resort. The dependability of the man was disconcerting. Islanders, particularly Kanakas, were notoriously undependable. They were late or didn't show at all. But Matisse was punctual. That quality in the man faintly disturbed Arch, but he couldn't understand why. He wanted to dislike Matisse. He'd every reason to dislike Matisse except one. The man had always been true to him. Loyalty was the single quality valued above all others in field intelligence work. Without loyalty there was no life.

The drive across Oahu took more than an hour. They came at Bellows from the Lanakai side, not the Waikiki side. The peak Arch was looking for was just across the main road leading in to the base. It was part of the Waimanalo area. Waimanalo was the worst island enclave for Kanakas on Oahu. A Haole could not walk the street on that small part of the island without being encountered by high threat locals. Most Haoles who were encountered never understood that the locals were all threat and no bite. The incidence of violence on Oahu was the lowest in the nation, while the incidence of car burglaries and petty theft was the highest.

Matisse decided to wait at the bottom of the peak, smoking *pakalolo,* what the locals on Oahu call marijuana. Not grown on the island, it was imported from the other islands where it was known by various powerful names for its kick. Matisse preferred purple Kona gold and smoked what he called a cigarette but was in reality something about the size of the cigar Bill Murray had smoked in Caddy shack.

It took an hour for Arch to reach the peak. The morning dew and earlier rains had made the going tough and slippery. Tea leaves covered the ground under the bigger unnamed vegetation around. Tea leaves were slippery when wet. Every step Arch gained had been followed by a short slide back. His OP shorts and Lauren polo shirt were totally soaked when he arrived at the peak, but the view was worth it. And the thermal action of swirling trade winds affected by the afternoon radiation of the sun was wonderful. The same effect that had propelled his glider thousands of feet into the air many years earlier served to cool and invigorate Arch in a most satisfying and comforting way. He wanted to plunge himself into finding out what was going on and not in thinking about Virginia.

Being at the top of the peak, which he's flown around and around many times in his youth but had never climbed, was euphoric. Swinging the Leica binoculars up to his eyes Arch was instantly transported. Back in time. To a mission of technological advancement in the Soviet Union. He was staring through the lenses down at an Ekranoplan Caspian Sea Monster. He was staring at an airplane. The airplane was stretched out on the refurbished sixty-two hundred foot runway that had not seen real air service since the Second World War, except for tiny gliders. The plane was the largest airplane ever to fly, by far, but it could only fly in ground effect. It wasn't a real airplane because it flew just a few tens of feet above ground or water. It weighed in at over a million pounds and flew with another million pounds of troops and supplies aboard. That amount could be the most part of an entire armored division. Arch had not seen one of the three prototypes he witnessed over twenty-five years before. But there it was, revealed by the remarkably clear German lenses. Somehow, at least one prototype of the huge aircraft had survived and astoundingly it was lying there on the old runaway right in front of him.

Arch sat back against the taro leaves and palm fronds propping him up in the filtering wind. He breathed in and out. The Ekranoplan. It was invented to transport huge amounts of men and armor across great distances. It had one fatal flaw. The eight huge jet turbines powering it ate fuel at a rate of ten tons of fuel per hour. Ten hours of three hundred mile an hour flight time was two hundred thousand pounds. No real long-range flights were possible because of the fuel-limited rand. Arch's mind turned cold. Unless the turbines were driven by fission generated steam. Then, given the size and power of the nuclear power plant, range might well be unlimited. With nuclear power, a plane of such size could deliver half a Marine division, in one unit to the opposite side of the earth in less than two days. Suddenly, the scintillation detector made sense.

The Apache caught his attention. Arch frowned in question. How could anyone know anyone was at the top of the peak, but somehow the approaching Apache helicopter seemed to know? That the Marine Corps had no such attack helicopters in its inventory would not even occur to Arch until later. The airborne beast came at him from high in the air, as if it knew exactly where he was concealed, nestled deep inside the green moist bracken. The Apache was a frightening mechanical beast, like a five-ton attacking wasp, except a whole lot more dangerous and deadly.

Arch fled. He slewed left and then right as he tried to find the trail down that he'd come up. He could find nothing in his panic. He'd seen the chain gun under the canopy of the Apache moving to direct its fire at him from under the things ugly snout. And then Arch lost all thought of the chopper and pursuit. He slid into a water sluice. A sluice was an artificial stream that was built to run straight down the side of the mountain. It captured him instantly and his body accelerated to near terminal velocity. Arch slid down the curved bottom of the sluice like a hot dog straight through a well-buttered bun. He continued to gain speed as he went, the air going his upturned face at such a speed that he had to unwillingly put his head back down or his eyelids would have been forced to open beyond their capability. Arch splashed out at the bottom of the sluice but did so into open air, flying five feet high with a large pond of water beneath him. He impacted butt first into a waiting ban of deep lava mud on the opposite side of the pond. It took ten minutes to work loose and then cover himself with brush. No chopper made its presence known. Arch lay encased in the mud for almost an hour, letting the panic bleed from his body and mind. His hand was a mess. The pain brought some recovering clarity to his mind.

There was a lot more to the Marine mission than just some Marine Corps experimentation or training exercise. Whatever was going on was big. Bigger than the Corps. Arch pulled himself free staggered through the mud to find Matisse sitting stoned in the bushes not far from the base of the mountain. However screwed up Matisse was, Arch was glad to see him. He dragged his own muddy body into the rear of the Bonneville.

"Home, Cheeves," he breathed, thoroughly exhausted, to Matisse. The islander laughed, and then floored the throttle of the over-torqued convertible. The car rocketed out of the bushes and onto the main road back toward Lanakai. In spite of the Apache, the revamped Soviet ground effects aircraft, and even the bizarre contretemps whatever the mission might be, Arch thought of Virginia. He'd come to the island for her. She was obviously way in over her head. He had to save her. Even if she was sleeping with the general.

VI

"Where we goin' boss?" Matisse yelled from the drivers seat, as Arch got into the old battered convertible. Matisse accelerated away so fast the huge single door on the passenger side slammed with the sound of gunshot.

"Cut back across the island," Arch instructed, with his damaged hand pushed against the dash and the other grasping the top of the door. "We'll use H3 and cross over the mountains. I need to get cleaned up somewhere between here and Ala Moana Shopping Center."

"We go Neiman Marcus? Cool. I love Niemen's. They usually won't let me in there." Matisse laughed some more, his THC level causing him to drive too fast and with too much abandon.

"What a shock," Arch murmured. "Potassium Iodide. We need that stuff for whatever they're leaking into the waters off Bellows. We can get it at Longs Drug Store, or what used to be Longs before CVS bought them. Unless they're sold out of the stuff." Arch thought about their prospects. Potassium Iodide overloaded the thyroid gland so it would simply reject any other iodine elements, including those that might be irradiated. Thyroid cancer was the most likely damaging result of sustained contact with low-level radiation. Potassium Iodide was about the only protection outside of a full Hazmat suit Arch could think of.

"A million tons. You said that plane was a million tons. No plane can be a million tons. An aircraft carrier isn't a million tons." Matisse threw the words back over his shoulder as they made their way toward the Kailua on-ramp to H3.

"A million pounds, not a million tons," Arch responded, mechanically, recalling the specifications of the huge plane. A million pounds gross and then another for the load. Whoever flew the plane in had to have flown it right in and just barely over the tops of the pines completely surrounding the airfield. Nobody was going to fly the monster thing out of there without cutting down a huge swath of pines to do it though. The runway was simply too short and the pines too high for such a large plane, even one flying only in ground effect, to make it. "They'll have to destroy much of the pine forest that makes Bellows so unique to do it," Arch said more to himself than to Matisse. None of it made any sense. The Marines didn't need to fly half a division anywhere. There were at least six U.S. Naval fleets at sea covering almost all of the oceans of the globe at any time. What could be the purpose of the large aircraft and how did it involve nuclear materials? Finally, how was it possible that there was some leakage from whatever nuclear materials were being used or stored?

"We get you cleaned up before we cross over," Matisse said. Without further comment he turned toward the Koolau Mountain Range and drove the big Pontiac to an automotive repair place near a housing development called Haiku plantations. Arch knew of the housing area from the Joseph Campbell 'Power of Myth' tapes. Joe had lived in Haiku and filmed the segments from his home there before passing on. The auto repair business had an outdoor shower. Arch rinsed himself thoroughly outside without undressing. He was wet but at least most of the mud was gone. His nailed hand was a mess but taking care of it would have to wait.

A large local in dirty overalls came out from under the sliding garage door, as Arch patted himself as dry as he could in the wind. The disheveled mechanic spoke a few words to Matisse and then went back inside.

"Why does an auto repair shop have an outside shower?" Arch asked Matisse, trying to brush his hair dry.

"Surf and come to work. Gotta get the salt off." Matisse answered using a tone of amazement, like everyone should know why an auto repair shop had an outside shower.

"Ala Moana," Arch instructed Matisse when he was about as dry as we was likely to get. His clothing remained more than damp but there was nothing to be done for it except pass some time. He climbed into the back seat of the Pontiac and Matisse did his usual high torque blast off. He sat up to dry himself off as much as he could, as Matisse guided the old Pontiac towards the huge shopping center on the other side of the island.

"We can't beat the CIA and the United States Marine Corps together," Arch murmured from his position lying in the sun across the Bonneville's wide back seat. "We just can't do it. They're too big. We'll end up dead or in Guantanamo."

Matisse drove the car well above any posted speed on the island taking H3's gentle curves with the Pontiac's ancient suspension maxed out and leaning far over through every turn. They penetrated one of the tunnels dug all the way through the Koolau range. After almost a full minute of near darkness the car burst out into sunshine on the leeward side of the island. The many-shaded and bright green beauty of the passing scenery only served to disguise Arch's miserable state of circumstance. Arch felt like they should be pulling over to purchase ether somewhere to more closely emulate the travels of Hunter S. Thompson so well described in his book called Fear and Loathing in Las Vegas.

They exited from H3 onto H1 heading from the Makai (seaward) direction toward Honolulu (toward Diamond Head). Oahu had its own directions. Towards the waters off of Waikiki was referred to as Makai. The inland mountains were in the opposite direction and called just that, while Diamond Head and Eva were used to describe the other two directions.

Ala Moana shopping center had once been the largest in the world, but had long ago been eclipsed by some water park place in Minnesota and then others around the continental United States. Ala Moana was still the largest in the islands and the underground parking was a nightmare. Getting in and out of the place without getting hit was considered an art form, while finding any kind of parking place at all was more a kindly gift from a merciful God. Matisse parked in a handicapped spot. Before Arch could complain the islander slapped a blue hanger onto the convertible's center mirror post.

"My grandma. No drive no more. Handicap sticka good for three more years though."

The drug store in the center, still called Longs although CVS purchased it some time back, had potassium iodide. Arch requested it from a skeptical pharmacist who eyed his damaged hand but he was able to buy six packages of six pills each. He bought a bottle of Fred drinking water because he liked the writing on the little bottle's label, and it was shaped like a pint flask so it more resembled a pint bottle of vodka than water. He downed a pill and then made Matisse take one. The drug would overload their thyroid glands so no radioactive iodine could get in if they were so exposed. He didn't bother explaining to his island associate anything further about why they might be needing to take such precautions. He picked up another throwaway cell phone from a stand next to the check out counter. He seemed to be losing cell phones like lizards in trouble lost tails.

The shoe place near the shopping center's performing stage had Teva sandals in his size. Finally, Arch didn't have to look like some Haole beach bum in bare feet. The trek up and slide down the mountain at Bellows had reminded Arch that his younger days of possessing solidly calloused feet were forever behind him. Somewhere on that slope his old Tevas would lay for a long time to come.

They went to the food court. Patty's Kitchen used to occupy a whole corner of the place but it was as dead and gone as Patty herself. Some Koreans now ran a faux Chinese food counter in its place. Arch and Matisse loaded up on local food from one of the other vendors. Lots of rice, soy sauce, pork hash and lomi lomi salmon. Arch ate pork hash while both of them sat at one of the small cheap tables stuffed into the center of the massive food court. Arch took out his phone and punched in some numbers.

"Who you calling?" Matisse asked. Arch ignored him while he finished off a chunk of the pork hash and waited for any answer.

Virginia answered after the sixth ring.

"Hello," Arch said, all of sudden unsure why he'd made the call at all, except he really had no one else to call who might help him understand what was going on.

"You insensitive jerk," Virginia yelled. Her voice was so loud Matisse sitting next to him heard the words.

"You seem to have trouble with women," Matisse whispered to Arch, before sucking down a huge chopstick load of soy-laden rice.

"Me? Insensitive?" Arch replied to Virginia's accusation, not believing his ears. "You set me up on the mission, had one of your henchman nearly kill me, and that was before having me tortured by some more of your people...not to mention sleeping with the married commander of the mission." Arch knew the last sentence he spoke was a mistake even before Virginia answered.

"You're beneath contempt..." she started, but Arch cut her off.

"Did you come straight from his bed to mine or was it the other way around?" He went on, unable to stop himself, Matisse looking over at him with an expression of twisted humor.

"You going steady with Virginia? Torture?" Matisse had stopped eating with his chopsticks half was to his mouth, staring down at Arch's poorly bandaged hand. "Your girl-friend torture you?"

Arch ignored Matisse, turning to notice the packed crowd of people they were among in the food court. People waited for an opening, sat, ate and then departed one after another. Although no one paid attention to anyone else on a cell phone the noise itself was difficult to deal with in trying to talk on the phone. Ordinarily. Virginia's voice level was so high however that she was easy to understand.

"I didn't do anything," she said. "I brought you here for this. I made sure we got back together again, no thanks to you."

Arch held the phone out in amazement, before gripping it back to his ear. "I came here on my own, and you somehow saw it to your own advantage to involve me in some deadly mission nobody will say one word about, even to others involved. One of your people almost killed me and when that didn't happen, I got three holes punched clean through my hand, plus an Apache helicopter almost finished me off over at Bellows. I came here to marry you not to get murdered by you."

There was a moment of silence on the other end of the phone. Finally, Virginia spoke again. "Marry me? Where the hell were you for fifteen years? You fell off the face of the planet. I brought you back to see if you'd built any character over the years. Any honor. But no, you're the same trouble-making machine of near total destruction you always were. I wouldn't marry you on a bet."

"Are you sleeping with him?" Arch asked. There was no answer to the question. Arch waited while Matisse sat grinning like a fool and nodding his head with one eyebrow raised and a smirk on his face.

"Was that a no?" Arch finally inquired hopefully into the silence, turning his back to Matisse. The phone went dead.

"Man, my wife never talk like that to me, or do that other stuff either," Matisse commented, going back to finishing his meal.

"She's not my wife," Arch replied, tersely.

"No matter," Matisse went on, "in Hawaii women know their place. My wife…"

"I don't care about your wife, and I don't like women who know their place, as you put it." Arch answered.

"I know, I know, I can tell from your talk with her," Matisse replied, 'but you should. My wife can find you a real woman who won't sleep with other men, not even if one is a general."

"Come on, we've got work to do," Arch said stiffly.

"Where we go now?" Matisse asked, dumping the remains of his food and mostly empty containers into a nearby trashcan.

"To the airport. I'm renting a real car. We can't drive around in that piece of junk and be taken seriously. We'll get a real car like a Lincoln or Cadillac, take it to Pearl Harbor and get a base sticker."

"Base sticker? How do you get one of those?" Matisse asked in a shocked tone.

Arch pulled out his wet wallet and retrieved a plastic card. "Officer's Military I.D. We'll get the sticker, patch my hand up at the Navy infirmary and get ready to go to the secure part of Bellows."

"Are you crazy?" Matisse said, stopping in his tracks. "They'll probably put us in jail when we show up at Pearl, much less at that special gate at Bellows."

"Nope," Arch said, flatly. "That's one of the problems related to very sensitive and compartmentalized missions. Nobody outside the mission usually knows a damned thing. This one is so secret that almost nobody inside the mission knows anything, as well. We'll be fine at Pearl, probably Bellows too. I'd be amazed if they don't just salute and wave us through the gate once we have the sticker. The I.D. is valid and the sticker will be good too."

"We'll? How you figure that we thing? I got no I.D. and no base sticker."

"Trunk. You'll be in the trunk, not that it might matter except for the fact that you look like a local island slime ball and that might raise suspicions."

"Trunk?" Matisse exclaimed. "I gotta ride in the trunk? That's evil man, and I thought you said that the CIA and the Marine Corps were just too big to fight. And I don't look local at all. You ever see a local driving a classic Pontiac convertible around?"

"You got me there," Arch answered, shaking his head. "And I said they're too big to beat, not too big to fight. Besides, the whole Marine Corps and the entire CIA aren't aware of this mission. Of that I'm certain. This thing is some sort of intense pocket operation probably run directly out of the White House. It has all the earmarks of White House stupidity written all over it. We might not beat whoever's involved but these people are sure going to know they were in a fight."

"And Virginia the bitch? Matisse asked, "what you going to do with her?

"She's in way over her head," Arch said back over his shoulder, as both men walked toward the Pontiac. "I can't save her from something I know almost nothing about. So let's find out what it's all about."

Matisse dragged his feet, following behind Arch until they got to the convertible. "Can't we just get a boat and go out to Rabbit Island? They got some fish and that terrible Angry Chameleon rum stuff from Kauai. We can drink that stuff out there and maybe forget this Virginia Haole bitch woman." Arch didn't answer. He simply got into the passenger seat of the Pontiac Matisse, looked straight ahead and waited. "This friendship between us could be another of those painful ones," Matisse concluded.

"Another?" Arch asked, as Matisse started the car.

"Yeah," Matisse answered, looking over his right shoulder as he backed the big Pontiac carefully from its small parking slot, "like the one between you and Virginia."

VII

The Hertz counter was empty when Arch went in to get a car more fitting than Matisse's Pontiac convertible. There were plenty of cars and Arch didn't bother to try to negotiate rates. A hundred dollars a day for a Cadillac, even if it wasn't as big as one of the old models. Arch missed the big Lincoln all the rental agencies carried at one time, but the days of those land giants were gone forever, except for relic jalopies like Matisse drove. Taking no chances Arch had Matisse wait for him in the Zippies parking lot at Hawaii Kai. Even the distinctive outrage of the Pontiac wouldn't be noticed in that busy place and they could leave it for quite some time before anyone might notice, if necessary.

Getting the base sticker was faster than finding the place that assigned them at Pearl Harbor. The days of Marine guards at Navy gates were gone with big cavernous trunked Lincolns and the private security guards supposedly guarding America's most secure bases were idiots, for the most part, even when it came to handing out the simplest of instructions. The question about what Arch wanted with a Pearl Harbor officer sticker for a rental car never came up. His I.D. said Brigadier General USMC and that about said it all under most military circumstances. The fact that he'd never really served as a general in any service was neither here nor there for most situations.

There was no Pearl Harbor infirmary. Arch had to leave through the Makalapa back gate of the base and head up to Tripler Hospital. The pain radiating from the nailed hand was too harsh and pervasive to ignore. They took him right away at the spic and span emergency room. After X-Ray, a diagnosis of no broken bones and little structural damage Arch was out of the place in two hours. Sixty stitches that would have to be taken out at some later date, a tight set of bandages and an arm sling Arch tossed in the garbage at the first opportunity got him out by early afternoon. He tossed the bottle of Ibuprofen in the same can he threw the sling into. The physician's assistant had arrogantly explained to him that although he claimed to be in a lot of pain his non-verbal behavior only supported a prescription of Ibuprofen. Arch passingly thought to put the woman on a mental list to be killed at some more appropriate time.

Matisse was right where he was supposed to be, as Arch had come to trust that he would be. Matisse was sitting at a booth near the Hawaii Kai harbor water nursing a giant soda when Arch walked up.

"Hey, brah," Matisse said with a great smile upon seeing him.

"Matisse," Arch responded obligingly, the local man again making him a bit uncomfortable with his expressive friendship and instant approval. "You ready?" he asked, sitting down across from the man with his back to the harbor.

Matisse sucked loudly from his drink container that obviously had no liquid left inside it. "Why you think the Virginia bitch Haole need to be saved? I thought you said it was her that got you into all this?"

Arch stared at his supposed new friend, wondering what made the man think in such circular ways. Trying to tell what Matisse was thinking was proving to be impossible. "She's not a bitch and don't call her a Haole. The "H" word is just that. And don't call me one either unless you want more trouble than you've already got. And finally, I'm not the only one in this. You were down in the same valley I was all taped up and ready to die."

"I know," Matisse said, resting his empty drink cup on the table between them but continuing to jostle the ice inside. "You save my life. That's why we friends for life."

"No," Arch corrected him, taking his good hand and jerking the empty cup from Matisse's. "We're friends only because nobody else will have you for a friend." Arch successfully tossed the cup into a nearby trash container almost ten feet away.

"Thank you," Matisse said, his smile dropping from his face.

"For what?" Arch asked in an exasperating tone.

Arch almost rolled his eyes but instead just looked at the mess of a local loser sitting across from him. Bits and small strips of duct tape goo still stuck to parts of his face and his clothes were a complete mess, but he was the only 'team' Arch had. Arch breathed in and out deeply. "She's into something she thinks she knows about but in reality knows nothing about. No matter how smart an agent is, and Virginia's very smart, there's no substitute for life experience. What's she's got herself into here is both off the books and dangerous."

"The radiation?" Matisse asked.

"No, nothing like that," Arch answered. I think whatever radiation we find will be rather inconsequential. The medication is just a precaution because I've been around that stuff before. You don't take chances with it. The Marines aren't stupid either.

They won't risk their own men unless they have to and in spite of the bizarre airplane thing I don't see why they would have to. This mission is one of those off the books kind of things that involves someone's personal agenda, and it's extremely dangerous because of what my partner did."

"He didn't do anything," Matisse said, spreading out both of his meaty hands over the table between them.

"That's just it. You don't understand what a big deal that was. He didn't stand for me. There is no mission first crap in working with the Agency. Partners always take care of partners no matter what. What he did, or didn't do, means that no other agent will ever work with him as a partner again. His field career is over, and he knows that. So why did he do it?"

"Some serious junk?" Matisse offered.

"Some serious junk indeed," Arch answered. "Let's hit it. I want to get aboard the base before the sun gets too low. Leave the Pontiac and we'll get it later. I'll put you in the trunk and then let you out when I find a safe place inside the wire."

The drive to Bellows was uneventful. The road to the base was along the coast and the drive one of the most spectacular in the world. The waves beat up from one of the deepest ocean trenches with the island of

Molokai in the distance. A constant booming spry of white was thrown up from the nearby cliffs and gawking tourists had to we watched out for as they veered to see natural wonders like the Blow Hole and Sandy Beach. The Caddy performed well although there were no demands placed on it simply because the non-stop continuous traffic permitted no performance driving at all.

As soon as Arch turned into the normally closed gate to Bellows, just past the Waimanolo Beach entrance he knew that nothing was going to work out as planned, not that he had any kind of real plan other than to show up and figure out how to gum up the works of whatever was going on. Not only was the gate closed but it was guarded by United States Marines. Arch couldn't avoid pulling up to the gate once he made the turn in. A corporal stood at attention and saluted the Pearl base sticker when Arch stopped the car before the small wooden gate guard.

"I.D., sir," the corporal requested, picking up a Bu-Pers (U.S. Bureau of Military Personnel) scanner with his left hand while holding out his right for Arch's card. Arch handed the card over and the corporal scanned it. He then stepped back and motioned with his free hand behind him. A staff sergeant appeared from nowhere.

"You have any paperwork, general?" he asked.

Arch understood instantly. He was in a "need to know," situation. Having proper I.D. was just the first step in such a situation. Have the proper clearance and then a written need to be there were the following and more definitive steps of the process.

"Just visiting from the mainland and I thought I'd come aboard to take in some beach and sun," Arch answered, lamely in his own opinion.

The staff sergeant was smooth as silk but firm as concrete.

"You can turn around right here and make your exit back to the main road. The base is currently closed to all non-essential personnel." He waved one hand in a circular fashion. The corporal handed Arch's I.D. back and salute again. Arch was dismissed.

Arch drove back to the Waimanalo Beach gate and found an empty parking place about as far from the beach itself as he could get. He looked around carefully before popping the trunk and letting Matisse out.

"Your fake I.D. not work, general?" Matisse asked, stretching his arms and back as if he'd been in the trunk for hours.

"It's not fake," Arch replied, slamming the trunk closed.

"You a real general?" Matisse went on, stopping his ridiculous stretching exercises.

"Not exactly," Arch responded. "We can't get on the base. I don't know how to proceed without getting on the base," he said, his tone despondent.

"What? Of course we can get on the base," Matisse said. "We go to the boat, go to Rabbit Island, wait for night, and then we land on the sand anywhere we want. They don't patrol the beach at night. Our people on Rabbit Island watch with binoculars."

"They have high technology gear. They don't need to patrol," Arch said, his voice depressed.

"So? We steal water from the base almost every night. They don't want us on Rabbit Island but they let us steal our water from them? I don't think so."

"Where's the boat and what's on the island," Arch said, staring out across the beach to the azure sea beyond. "I can see the damned thing out there from here. There's nothing there. Magnum P.I. island. Nobody goes there."

"Back side," Matisse replied, looking out to the breathtaking island in the distance. "Brilliant idea we occupy. The Department of Natural Resources has no amphibious stuff. We safe.

"Yeah, right," Arch laughed out. "Like the governor can't call up the Marine National Guard anytime he wants. They might just have an amphibious capability."

"Boat's near Sea Life Park by Makapuu," Matisse said, point toward Diamond Head way.

Arch drove in the traffic back the way they'd come. The boat proved to be a battered and patched Zodiac in such bad condition Arch thought it might never make it through any seas, much less out in the open ocean. Matisse read his expression. "We get to use boat and the park people make believe we don't exist as long as we bring it back."

"I don't want to know," Arch said, is attitude still near rock bottom.

Matisse guided the boat away from the pier that stuck out from near the entrance to the park. The water proved to be choppy but no threat to the Zodiac's limited capability. The old Evinrude outboard that drove the boat sputtered and backfired but held up until they reached the only sandy beach on the island. "They can see us land because it's only rocks on the other side," Matisse stated, killing the motor. "I'll have one of the Bruddas drive it back for supplies."

Arch frowned but said nothing. What were they supposed to do without a boat?

Both men climbed the mountain using an old and little used winding path back from the very peak. Just over the top they came upon a small collection of blue plastic covers held up my tent poles. The whole mess of wind-flapping plastic sounded like a bunch of kids passing on bicycles with baseball cards clipped to their wheels.

Matisse's small band of locals, five men and three women looked a bit bedraggled to Arch but he allowed himself to be introduced around.

"What's the plan?" he asked of Matisse when they finally broke free to stand just beyond the top of the ridge and view Bellows Beach stretched out before them.

"Tonight we cross to beach under cover of darkness," Matisse whispered into the wind so quietly that Arch almost couldn't make out what he said.

"Cover of darkness? Where do you get that crap, from the movies? What do we use for a boat," he went on scanning the island in every direction for sign of something capable of putting them ashore in surf conditions.

"No boat," Matisse replied, like the conclusion was self-evident. "We swim. You must swim good. You raised out here like local. You pass CIA swimming tests."

"Jesus Christ," Arch said in disgust. "Swim? It's over a mile and we've got to come through surf to get on the beach. I can swim that far but the water looks treacherous as hell."

"Water just choppy because reef not far below," Matisse said, pointing over the ridge at a distinct line of deep blue and light blue. There were only large slightly breaking swells in the deep blue field of view. "As soon as we cross reef, I mean. See, reef only about four hundred yards off. Only have to worry about sharks in the deep water. They don't swim over or inside reef."

"Sharks? Sharks? You've got to be kidding me," Arch replied, his disbelief evident in his expression and tone.

"No worry," Matisse said. "I swim many times. Never bitten once. Only seen sharks a few times and they stayed away. Jelly fish bigger worry."

"Jelly fish? What?" Arch's voice began to rise in tone as he spoke. "I'm allergic to Jelly fish venom."

"Good and bad news, boss," Matisse said, somehow adopting the title 'boss' in addressing Arch. "Good news is full moon gone so hard to see us. Bad news is just past eight days gone and that's when the jelly fish come out."

"What was the good news again?" Arch asked, acidly.

"No worries, I told you," Matisse said in a calming voice. "We have rash guards to wear. Like wet suit but thinner. Guard against stings."

"Rash guards," Arch repeated in a low disgusted tone. "Over a mile swim through shark and jelly fish infested waters to arrive through pounding surf onto a beach that we're supposed to get across unseen and search through a pine forest to discover something we don't know anything about."

"Yes boss," Matisse grinned. "We have great adventure."

Arch's shoulders sagged, as he turned to follow his new friend back to the flapping plastic tents to await the coming of night and to get into whatever rash guards were.

VIII

The rash guards weren't so bad, Arch decided, wishing he had a vanity mirror to check himself out in. Like a wetsuit, but better because the thin elastic long sleeve top and bottoms held everything in without giving him a feeling of being compressed. He knew he'd lost ten ponds in appearance alone. He sat and waiting while the sun slowly set over the deep blue beating sea fully on display from the back side of Rabbit Island. Molokai lay twenty miles, or so in the distance, its narrow east facing side fully visible because it was the eastern coast from which arose the highest cliff top to sea surface distance in the world. Rising up well over three thousand feet the cliffs would be visible until the sun was fully set.

"Matisse, let me use your cell phone," Arch said, holding out his right hand.

Matisse wore only swimming trunks and a Dark Quicksilver sweatshirt. Although he'd provided the rash guards to Arch there'd been nothing available that would cover his short but incredibly thick torso.

"How you like sandals?" he asked Arch, handing over his phone, "and why you note use own phone?"

Arch looked down at his blue feet while absently accepting the phone.

"They're not sandals. They're shoes, reef runner shoes called Hydro Kick Backs," he replied, knowing the heavy callouses on Matisse's bare feet would need no such protection, but surprised that someone had thought of his own. The light canvas tops covering hard rubber soles were made by a local rapidly growing local company called Alukai He punched numbers into the cell phone before bringing it up to his right ear. "I can't use my phone or they'll know instantly exactly where we are, not that these tents are much protection from look down satellite equipment in use today." After almost a full minute he hit a button and handed the phone back to Matisse. "Not answering, at least not to your caller I.D. number. I'm not leaving a message. She'd just give them your cell data, which she might do anyway."

The phone rang. Arch reached back toward Matisse but the islander held up his free hand. "It's the Haole bitch, calling back all aright."

Arch stepped forward and took the iPhone from the man's hand.

"Virginia?" he asked.

"What do you want and where are you," Virginia responded, "and who's phone are you calling from.

You're a fugitive from justice. Where are you and what are you trying to pull?"

Arch looked at the phone briefly, shot a nasty look at Matisse for turning on the speaker, but answered without turning it off.

"What's that noise?" Virginia asked before he could get anything out.

"Just the wind," Arch replied, weakly, which was the truth. Instead of dying down as the sunset, which was normal for the trades blowing over the Hawaiian Island chain, the wind seemed to be increasing.

"Hi, Virginia," Matisse yelled at the phone with cupped hands, then started laughing to himself so hard he had to bend over.

"Who's that?" Virginia asked, "are you in a local bar?"

Arch grimaced and then turned his back to Matisse and walked outside of the tent. The madly flapping edges of the tent sounded like machine gun fire so he moved as far away from the place as he could go without getting too close to the edge of the cliff. The wind still gave off so much noise as it twisted and swirled over the lip that it was difficult to near anything else. Matisse followed him outside.

"You have no clue what your involved with and I'm going to find out. You don't work in the field," Arch yelled into the end of the phone. "You only command agents like me to do your bidding. We don't tell you what it's really like at all. I'm going to save you from something you don't understand."

"You're an idiot," Virginia said, her voice thin and breaking up in the wind.

"Idiot? I'm an idiot?" Arch almost screamed to be heard. "You know better than that. I've never failed you once on any mission."

"Not on any mission," Virginia instantly replied with acid from each delayed word.

"Alright, I'll quit right now if you tell me you don't love me," Arch said, more softly but with deep feeling. After a few seconds the line went dead.

"We not going?" Matisse asked, gently taking his phone from Arch's clenched fingers.

"What do you mean?" Arch responded with amazement. "She didn't say she didn't love me. That means she loves me. We've got to go. We've got to find out. What about the radiation? The pollution? The Hawaiian Sovereignty cause you support?"

"Man, the line went dead. She didn't say anything."

"I know her," Arch said, turning to face back into the building wind. White caps covered the roiling tumbling waters stretching across some of the most treacherous seas in the world. The narrow stretch of water between Molokai and Oahu was almost seven thousand feet deep. Waves crisscrossed, coming from every direction, as the big long fetch swells of the North Pacific were broken and redirected by their encounter with the islands.

"How long do we wait?" Arch asked Matisse.

"A few hours," Matisse answered, moving to the cliff and sitting down to dangle his feet dangerously above the sea breaking heavily a few hundred feet below. "The most dangerous thing about all this isn't the jelly fish, the sharks, the surf, the reef or the swim. It's that Haole bitch. I can just feel it."

Arch sat down a few feet behind Matisse to watch the sun slowly make its way below the distant horizon. "You know, you can always bail out on this thing. I was a Boy Scout camping on that beach many years ago. I can go it alone," Arch said, into Matisse's back and blowing wind.

"I've gotta go brudda. They're my tribe. I gotta take care of them like you want to stupidly take care of the Haole bitch."

"Your tribe?" Arch exclaimed, quietly. "They don't even talk to you and according to you I'm your only friend and I barely know you."

"They don't have to be my friends. They are there for me and I'm there for them. It's the local deal. Besides, I got nothing else going on. Sixty-four dollars, my Pontiac, a cell phone and I'm not much living anywhere at the moment either. Under the pines at Sherwood Forest look pretty good to me right now."

"Sherwood Forest," Arch answered, wistfully. "I haven't heard that phrase used in a long time. "They still take from the rich and give to the poor at Bellows?"

"Nah, all that went away when this high security shit came to the area," Matisse said, turning so Arch could make our his words more clearly.

The public, meaning my people, get to use a little bitty piece of the beach but only on weekends and theirs no parking anymore. Used to be we could park under the pines or on the beach even. Now they have big rocks blocking everything. And video cameras everywhere. No more local fun."

Arch got up to walk back toward the sand ridge on the other side of the flapping blue ten complex. He stared at the full stretch of Bellows Beach little more than a mile and a half over the chopping water. It was beautiful, back by multi-green colored foliage of all densities and description. The pines just back from the nearly white sand were achingly attractive until you looked up. The western side of the Koolau Mountain Range was simply breathtaking, especially with the fading rays of light bouncing up from the flora. The entire scene was almost artificial it was so beautiful. He thought about what he was trying to do. There was no longer any mission, if there ever was. In fact, he was planning on doing the same thing Matisse had been doing when the sky fell on him. Could Arch hope to threaten the government to the extent that they'd leave Virginia alone any more successfully than Matisse had threatened the federal judge? It didn't seem likely. Matisse was an ignorant citizen and Arch was a player but that didn't' necessarily change anything. There was more firepower in a single Apache helicopter than Arch, Matisse and the entire Hawaiian Sovereignty Movement could bring to bear in a lifetime. Who was he kidding? Virginia was about to become as expendable as he himself, Matisse and the rest of them already had. The Hawaiians would no doubt already be dead from the "collateral" effects of drone Hellfire missiles except that Rabbit Island was such a visible beloved part of one of America's most populated vacation destinations.

Arch entered one of the tents and was promptly handed a small plastic bowl filled with raw fish chunks. Poke. The word was pronounced PO-Kay, and it was a local Hawaiian staple. Ahi tuna was offloaded from local fishing boats where the best of it was filleted and cut into chunks. The chunks of fresh fish were marinated in a few ounces of Aloha Soy Sauce, a bit of ginger and the Hawaiian version of monosodium glutamate called Aginomoto. "Poke," the woman said in handing him the bowl. "You need um energy for um swim. Eat all."

Arch took the bowl out into the near dark beyond. There were not implements. He ate the chunks with his fingers and then cleaned the bowl and his hands in a nearby dune of blowing sand nearby. Although he'd eaten plenty of sashimi and sushi over the years no fish tasted better than local Hawaiian poke.

After dark, with only the waning gibbous slice of the moon offering any light at all, Arch and Matisse made there way down the winding but well worn path to the only possible landing or launching spot on the small island. A near perfect small horseshow beach appeared as they made their way through the final high scrub and bracken. The small island received only a small bit of the rain normal to Bellows only a mile or so away. The plant growth dry and brown in full daylight. On each of their backs were taped large clear plastic bags with clothing, wallets and cell phones inside. Arch carried the sim card to his iPhone in his wallet although he'd come to believe that any Apple product could be tracked by the government no matter what was done to it short of grinding it up on some junkyard disposal.

The water was cool at first but then warm with the wind blowing across its calm surface seeming almost frigid on their heads shoulders. They breast stroked out beyond the cover into rough water. The swells rose and fell all around them, tossing both men up and around. It took their full attention to keep their heads clear of the white caps foam tops and stay on course toward the lower end of Bellows. The plan was to land on that part of the beach normally used by the locals on the weekend and almost entirely avoided by the military at all other times. Matisse knew that area of the beach and interior foliage and trees well while Arch had clear memories of romping through almost all the rest of the base when he was in his early school years. The plan was to be on the beach in less than an hour.

What could go wrong, except for jellyfish and sharks, did go wrong. The tide was too low once they reached it. Both men were near sea sick from the constant jousting with the outer reef waters when they cross onto the reef. Much smaller waves, most less than two feet high, swashed across the quarter mile thick reef. They could not lie down and ride over the reef and they couldn't' get up and walk. The crabbed from one coral head, barely below the surface until struck by an incoming wave, to another a few yards away. It was the only way they could avoid serious injury. Neither man had been able to speak during the rough water crossing. Sharing a coral head and waiting for another wave set to pass gave them enough time and condition to speak.

"Man, you one tough Haole," Matisse gasped out. "This kinda swim is awful. How you do it?"

"Conditioning and luck. I'm lighter than you. I float higher. We should have worn gloves and these rash guards are no match for the coral."

They moved together but to different coral heads, once more waiting for another bigger set to wash over them, hoping they'd be able to hold on. Coral cuts, no matter how light, were extremely painful and almost always infected. They worked ever slower to clear the reef as the waves seemed to get higher and higher.

"Tide going up," Matisse whispered over to Arch from ten yards away between sets. "Waves clearing the reef soon and then higher surf inside."

"Any more good news?" Arch shot back.

"Keep your voice down," Matisse force whispered back.

"Voice down?" Arch yelled back, laughing out loud. "Why, are we the only idiots to be dumb enough to be out here in the middle of the night?

A wave washed Matisse from his perch. Arch watched him wash away and then disappear. He gentled himself down onto the surface of the water into the rising trough of another incoming way. He surfed along with it, more inside the water than riding the outside. Suddenly, he plunged over a small waterfall. They were inside the reef. Both men paddled together but there was no celebration. Both men were nearly exhausted and they had the surf line to deal with after a half-mile swim.

The surf line proved to be no challenge once they'd negotiate the water in between. The swells were running to five feet but the waves had no real power once they broke. The inside break was worse than the outside one simply because there was an inshore hole. Both men got stuck in the hold and had to swim down the beach until they could clear it where a small creek, bordering the edge of the base, exited out into the open ocean.

Arch checked his Breguet watch. It had taken them three hours to travel little more than a mile. Both men lay on the sand, battered, cut up and too tired to crawl under the pines without rest. Arch crawled forward. He knew their bodies would register as black objects against the reflected near white of the soft sand. They'd also register that way on any night vision device, if anyone were bothering to look. Marines never took security lightly, especially when it came to protecting their own property and space. The Marine Corps was notorious for stealing equipment from other services while they made stealing from the Corps next to impossible.

The plan had been to get securely and deeply in among the pines just off the beach area. There both men would freshen up using the stream water, dry off as best they could and get their clothing on. From there they'd proceed inland toward the high security to see where they could get over or under the barbwire fence. It was a plan of simplicity depending upon substantial amounts of serendipity and it never got off the ground. Arch and Matisse made it in under the pines, took another break and did not wake up until dawn. The swim had done them in.

Arch woke up first, almost instantly realizing he'd not awakened from the sound of the surf but from another sound much louder and more threatening. He hit Matisse on the shoulder and jumped to his knees, turning to face back toward the water they'd come out of only hours before.

"What's that?" Matisse got out, crawling out from under the big pine they'd slept under. Arch followed. Both men stood standing in the same attire they'd arrived in earlier, watching a big flat air boat sweep in over the reef and head directly toward their position.

"What is it?" Matisse asked, in wonder.

"LCAC, land craft air cushion," Arch answered in a despondent voice.

The hovercraft, capable of carrying sixty tons of men and equipment took only seconds to cross the water from the reef to the sand. Once there it swept huge billowing clouds of sand upward, stopped and then settled into a whining near silence. A wide front door began to swing down from the gray hovercraft.

"Cool," Matisse said, almost in a whisper. "It's like the War of the Worlds. What's in it? What's gonna come out? Why is it here?"

"I think we got their attention," Arch responded, gathering his unopened plastic bag together and beginning to walk toward the vehicle.

Matisse ran to catch up with him in the soft sand. "We going to check it out?" he said, his voice excited.

"I guess you might say that," Arch replied, watching a full company of Marines beginning to run outward from the hovercraft, already beginning to form a growing perimeter that would soon include them.

The Marines came out of the hovercraft hatch at a run, racing toward Matisse and Arch. Both men stood too stunned to move. The Marines came within a few feet of them and then split to run right by. From just beyond where they stood the Marines pealed off and formed what resembled a fast opening flower. In only a few seconds they were surrounded, the Marines settling in with their weapons pointed outward, as if to defend them from some unknown enemy.

A single officer walked out of the hovercraft and made his way slowly toward Arch and Matisse. He stopped when he was a few feet away, and then saluted. He was wearing silver captain's bars on his combat utilities and two black bars held by Velcro to the center of his helmet.

He snapped his right hand to his side and said only one word: "Gentlemen." He waited at a position of attention.

"What's the deal captain," Arch said, when it appeared the neither the captain or anybody else was going to say anything further.

"Well sir, it would appear that General Crow would like to announce his compliments and invite you for a short visit at his quarters up near the secure part of this base," the captain replied with a smile, although he maintained his position of attention.

"Stand at ease," Arch ordered. "Why the drama?"

"What drama, sir?" the captain replied, relaxing his body and coming to a loose parade rest position.

"The drama of your difficult swim into the beach in the dark or the landing of our amphibious vehicle?"

Arch got the Marine humor realizing there was no way he and Matisse could have drowned or much else without a bunch of Navy Seals dropping from the sky to rescue them. Their travel from Rabbit Island had no doubt been recorded in detail real time and the subject of considerable humor.

"All this to take us less than half a mile up the beach," Arch said, smiling back at the captain. "You didn't need guns and a hovercraft battle ship for that."

"Actually, my orders were to transport you with full security if you agree," the captain replied. "Mike Company is here for your protection. You aren't being forced to do anything. The general is asking for an audience. You have full freedom to reply as you wish although once you leave Bellows we would no longer be able to provide security. What's your pleasure, sir?" The Marine returned to a noticeable position of attention.

"Maybe they give us ride back to the island?" Matisse said, hopefully, his eyes round and large as they continued to take in the Marines, machine guns and the huge monster of a landing craft.

"Do we get to keep our weapons?" Arch asked,

"Absolutely, sir," the captain responded, instantly

"You know we don't have any weapons, don't you?" Arch said, with a sigh.

"Yes, sir," the Marine answered, with no change of expression, his smile long gone.

"Cell phones?" Arch continued.

"Of course, sir. Suppressed, however," the captain actually seemed sympathetic about that.

"My I.D. still good?" Arch finished.

"Which one?" the captain replied, his small nearly invisible smile returning.

"We walk up the beach?" Arch pointed, there being no reason he could think of to test the captain's word. Oahu was all of five hundred and ninety square miles. There really were almost no place to hide for any length of time, not from the CIA and the Marines.

"Of course not, sir," the captain snapped, immediately pulling out a small radio and keying in some code. In only a few seconds a battle command Humvee pulled under the trees and made its way through the soft sand like it was built for just such a mission, which it was.

"What's going to happen?" Matisse whispered to Arch, as the vehicle drove through a break the Marines made for it in their defensive perimeter. The defensive ring closed as soon as the Humvee was through.

Arch looked over at the frightened Hawaiian before approaching the back door of the truck, already swinging open to accept them. "Saying I don't know would be a huge understatement, but I've got a feeling that you are about to be my only friend for quite some time to come."

IX

The Humvee proved to be empty, an enlisted Marine wearing no rank exiting the vehicle as Matisse and Arch got in. The heavy armored door slammed shut and the driver took off. There was nobody else in the Humvee.

Arch looked through the bulletproof glass, as they four-wheeled over the packed pine needles to the road. The scenery was surreal to him. It was exactly the same and in exactly the same small area he'd camped with his Boy Scout troop so many years before. He'd been afraid of snakes and nobody could tell him that there were no snakes in the Hawaiian Islands. Only the coming of the completely sewn in canvas bottoms to scout tents, and zippered mosquito nets, had allowed him to sleep the nights through without constantly waking to check for slithering monsters. The only benefit of having such an irrational fear had paid him was that he alone, other than Torres, the scoutmaster, had had his own tent.

"General's quarters down at the end of the base?" Arch inquired of the driver, not necessarily believing the company commander back at the big hovercraft.

"Sir," was all the Marine replied, his voice cut off and terse, as if the last thing he wanted was any dialogue with the two he was carrying in the back seat.

"Why all the guns facing out back there?" Matisse asked Arch. "What were they guarding us from? Is somebody other than them after us, or what?"

"Intimidation," Arch answered, with a knowing smile. "Didn't you feel it? A display of power and force. Shock and awe. Indirect threats are sometimes much more effective than direct threats. Didn't phase you a bit though, did it?"

"Nah," Matisse replied, softly. "What's going to happen now?"

"Whatever they want to happen. I guess it was that way from the start but missions never go the way they're supposed to so I'm counting on some serendipity to help."

"Serendipity? That doesn't sound so good," Matisse said.

The Humvee was doing no more than fifteen miles an hour so the trip took more than just the few minutes it would have taken if they'd been making any kind of reasonable speed. Arch thought they might be experiencing more intimidation but he wasn't sure. The whole thing, whatever it was, just didn't seem to have that kind of advance planning or experienced players at work. The Marines landing from the hovercraft had been regular Marines except for their lack of rank markings. It just didn't seem that Arch and Matisse, no matter what they might do, could be important enough to spend much time or assets over.

The Humvee didn't slow for the gate guards, much less stop. The guards didn't wave or acknowledge the vehicle's passing except to stare as it went by. The base had changed. There were no off duty personnel swimming, getting gas at the on base station or even hanging about the many small rental cabins maintained by the Air Force for any active duty or retired military personnel who might want to avoid the outrageous room rates charged in Waikiki. The road ended at the base of a rather laid back looking home constructed almost entirely of fitted black lava rocks held together by mixed concrete, like many of the local walls to be found around all the islands. The Marine stopped the vehicle and waited. Matisse and Arch climbed out. The Humvee departed with both rear doors swinging shut due to the acceleration force of the departing vehicle. The Marine driver was obviously returning to his duty station at a much higher rate of speed than he'd used to deliver his charges.

"I guess we knock?" Matisse asked, approaching the single barred gate set deeply into the stone. There was a small courtyard beyond the bars but no one there.

"Enter," a tinny voice said, emitted by a small speaker set at head height by the edge of gate. The door buzzed open a few inches.

"Cool," Matisse said, and then pushed the gate fully open.

Arch looked around for a rock to prop the door open. There were no loose rocks so he grabbed a nearby bench and put it in the gap so the door couldn't close after them.

They climbed some steps, and then turned a corner and had to climb some more. Arch didn't slow or turn when he heard the gate behind them snap shut with a loud click. Evidently there were personnel somewhere unseen in the courtyard, probably stationed there for the specific purpose of making sure whoever came in was supposed to be in and whoever was in was staying until dismissed. There would be no quick rush out of the residence to make an escape, but then Arch hadn't expected any.

Arch knocked on the Koa wood door with his undamaged right hand. Koa was so rich, rare and expensive it would only have been used years earlier for something as plain as a door leading into a military officer's cottage. The door opened but no one appeared to have opened it. Arch stepped in with Matisse crowding behind him. Arch looked behind the door but there was nobody there or anywhere in the great room. He looked back at the door latch as he swung it closed. Electrically operated. The door clicked shut with a slight but distinctive electrical sound.

The general's visiting quarters were as Arch had seen at other bases but much more opulent, and there was certainly no other set of quarters with a similar view of such tropical magnificence. One set of great room windows faced the other windward side of the island, taking in the full view of Lanakai, all the way to where Kaneohe Marine Base lay if you knew it was there. The other wall of windows gave a full view down Bellows Beach all the way past Waimanaolo to Makapuu Point where an old lighthouse now attracted photographers and tourists of all kinds. Rabbit Island sat placidly offshore, brilliantly lit up by the morning sun. The island was too far away to note any activity or the presence of any of the Hawaiians occupying it.

The general's view was like no other on Oahu.

A Marine Officer appeared from around a hidden corner near the back of the room. He was a captain, wearing a Class B uniform, tropical attire (short sleeve khaki shirt with green trousers without stripe), sporting a leather belt with cross belt running over his shoulder. A pistol holster swung gently from the belt as he walked. Because he was under arms he also wore a piss cutter green cover (narrow hat running from forehead to the back of his neck). He carried a file over to a broad table near the window overlooking the La-nakai facing side of the home. He set the folder down and then looked up, as if noticing Arch and Matisse for the first time.

"Gentlemen, I'm captain Star and I'm the general's aide. The general will see you forthwith. I will ask you not to touch the materials I'm leaving for his attention as I make my own exit." The aide walked out of the room the way he'd walked in. Arch noted the Cor-fam (crummy artificially polished black shoes instead of the real spit shined ones) with nearly silent rubber soles and the man's West Point ring that had flashed in the early morning sun.

"Stuffy prick, with the name star to go with the general's, no doubt," Arch murmured, walking toward the table.

"Haole prick," Matisse whispered at about the same time. "Sorry," he followed up with to Arch, al-most immediately.

"For which part?" Arch returned, absently, as he took in the NSA folder with his own name on it. He stood staring down at the half-inch thick file, trying to decide whether to open it or not. He had little doubt that he and Matisse were under full surveillance but what did it matter at that point.

A man's deep voice spoke before his hand could reach the table.

"Gentlemen," the voice said. Matisse and Arch turned as one.

A tall, nearly gaunt man of middle age walked toward them. He wore the same uniform as his aide but without the armament, belt or cover. The only mark of his rank was a single gold star pinned to the exact center of his khaki shirt collar tips. The front pleats running up and down each side of the shirt looked so sharp they could cut skin if not handled gently. He also wore a West Point ring, although where the captain's had been gold with black onyx, Point colors, the general's was white gold with a huge diamond in the center.

He sat down without saying anything else and opened the file to its first page, which had the word SECRET slanted across it in large red letters.

"General DeWare, I presume," Arch said, taking a seat across from the Marine Officer. Matisse leaned against the back of a couch just behind him.

"And who or what you are is, apparently, not to be known, unless you are going to be kind enough to enlighten me," the general said, beginning to leaf through the NSA file. Arch could not help but stare. He'd never seen a real honest to God NSA file in his career, much less his own file. How a hard copy file from that secretive agency came to be in the general's possession all the way out on Oahu was a complete mystery to him, but it again caused him to think that something vitally serious was going on that nobody outside the mission had any clue about.

"You're a general yourself," DeWare said, "or maybe not. You've been a lot of Marine Corps ranks, I note. In fact, you were a major before you were a captain, and that's not really possible...but here it is. No Command and Staff College. How can you be a general without that? You can't, but here it is and here you are." DeWare closed the file. "It doesn't matter, I suppose. What you, and your local trash friend, are is trouble."

"Trouble?" Arch blurted out. "You think you're the only one here sleeping with Virginia Westray? Talk about trouble."

The general simply stared across the table, first at Arch and than at Matisse. His face, then his whole head, turned a beet red and his right hand began to tremble slightly.

The general's movement reminded Arch of the pain in his own hand. Without saying anything further he slipped his left hand into his pocket, took out a few Ibuprofen tablets and popped them into his mouth. He looked up at the general. Mr. Perfect came to his mind. The man was totally in the moment and wearing everything, including his role, to perfection. General Perfect.

"Get out and stay out," the perfect general said, his voice low, his words delivered with a near hiss. "You get involved in this and nobody will be able to save you. You were called in to do something and you did it. Now go home. Haiku has nothing to do with you, and as far as Virginia is concerned, and we have talked about you, you are nothing more or less than an aged child, and not a good child at that." General DeWare stood up, put Arch's file under his right arm and started to walk toward the back of the room.

"You've got Virginia tied up in something she's not ready for and you need to let her go if you care about her," Arch said to the general's back, knowing the words were probably futile.

"You're out of here. These men will take you back to town. Sit there, drink there, stay there and then fly out. If your local scum friend goes back to Rabbit Island he'll be snuffed out like his pals, never to see the light of day again." General DeWare stopped and turned, "and you general, major, warrant officer or whatever the hell you are, gave us all we need to make that happen."

Two men came around the panel's edge, as the general disappeared. "Hey guys," one of the men said, waving a Taser toward them. Lorrie and Kurt were back.

Arch stood up and backed toward Matisse until his back was against the couch too.

"Oh, don't look so surprised, we're in and you're out," Lorrie noted. "Simple, really. Kurt here would love to get even for his hand. He gestured toward his injured companion.

"Get even, get even?" Arch asked, holding up his bandaged hand.

"He nailed my hand first. You broke bones," Lorrie noted. "You spilt blood. There was supposed to be no blood, if you will recall overhearing. But never mind. We're not here about that. We're here to escort you to your carriage, that more resembles a pumpkin than a carriage." Lorrie motioned with the Taser. Kurt glared but said nothing, his damaged hand splayed and stretched with wires held together using little nuts and bolts. Lorrie approached Arch and Matisse until he was standing only a few feet away. Kurt held back, his good hand noticeably positioned behind his back. Suddenly, Lorrie smashed the Taser down on Arch's injured hand that lay resting gently on the couch back.

Arch almost crumpled to the floor in pain, letting out a strangled moan. He pulled the hand close to his body, feeling the bleeding begin to seep through the light bandage. He struggled to control himself as Kurt spoke for the first time.

"How's that feel, Mr. hot-shot tough-guy international man of mystery?"

Matisse grabbed Arch around the shoulders and eased him back the way they'd come. Sitting on the other side of the open gate at the bottom of the final set of steps was Matisse's Pontiac.

"Found this pumpkin down the way a bit, and thought you'd be more at home than the Caddy," Lorrie said, standing well in front of Kurt just back from the gate. "Hope to see you soon. Kurt doesn't talk much but he'll be most happy to see you if you turn up again."

Arch eased slowly into the front seat of the Bonneville and then went to work trying to re-position the bloody bandages wrapped around his damaged hand.

"Moana. Head for the Moana," Arch ordered Matisse, barely able to speak.

"You think you going to bring that Haole woman to the Moana?" Matisse asked. "I know what you thinking. You going to trust her again? Those guys who keep hurting you work for your Agency. For her. Not for the scarecrow general. I don't think she be much of a good woman, and you don't have that many hands."

Arch finished working on his hand before he responded. "You can drop the local Wahini stuff. You don't know a thing about Virginia, or me for that matter. I don't want some woman that takes my crap all the time. I want intellect, independence and some kind of equal partner. Virginia has always stood up for me, not matter how she seems to act or what she says. Somehow, she works on my best behalf even when it looks like she isn't."

Matisse looked over at Arch for too long to be driving the way he was. "You in love with that woman. You got it bad. Shaka brah. She's dangerous. I'm afraid of her and I haven't even met her. But you my brah and I back my brah."

They drove without speaking to downtown Waikiki. Matisse put some oldies station on the ancient single speaker radio. "Sherry, Sherry baby, Sherry can you come out tonight..." played with surprising strength, with Frankie Valli belting it out and the cavernous car interior with the top up magnifying his voice. Matisse parked free at the Royal Hawaiian, not far from the Moana, where the doorman was part of his sovereignty group. The hotel was painted an awful pink but the interior breathed with a quiet old island style of quiet class as they walked through the lobby.

Kalakaua, the main drag through Waikiki, was packed, but then it was always packed unless it was three in the morning. They walked straight through the Royal and shopping complex toward the Moana. What was left of the International Market Place was their first destination just across from the Moana. About every product in the jammed space was sold from wheeled sales carts. It was like a hugely wide alley in downtown Hong Kong. And every cart sold the same tourist junk, from phony jade to Zippo lighters and cheap bangle bracelets. An old drug store still functioned, with only Japanese characters to give away the fact that it dispensed anything but the other local crap around it. Arch loaded up on bandages and used two hundred in cash to convince the old man behind the counter to give him some codeine powder; the kind Japanese people could buy for a song in Tokyo without any doctor's permission.

Matisse guarded the door to a lobby bathroom while Arch went inside to do the best he could on his hand with the materials they'd purchased. Finally, he had to call the Hawaiian in because he couldn't wrap the hand effectively without help.

"Let's go get a drink," Arch said, wading through the crowd with Matisse trailing behind, carrying the bag with the rest of the medical supplies. The Moana had been redone some years back. They walked through the elegant lobby and out onto the back veranda. Arch stared up at the huge banyan tree that had been a fixture of wonder ever since his childhood. At one time there'd been a brass plaque indicating that Robert Lewis Stevenson had penned Treasure Island under it but no one could recall what happened to the plaque or whether what was written on it was true.

They got lucky and found an empty table near the sand. The small gentle waves of Waikiki Beach lapped pleasantly nearby. Arch looked at the bar Pupu menu but didn't get far before one word came back to his mind. A waiter came over and Arch ordered two Mai Tai drinks. He knew they'd cost almost twenty bucks apiece but he intended to dust his own liberally with the codeine powder.

"Haiku," Arch said, off a sudden. "Our perfect general mentioned Haiku. What could Haiku be?" Arch said the words aloud, more to himself than to Matisse.

"Haiku Plantations or Haiku Gardens on the other side," Matisse answered, checking out the PuPu menu for himself. Then he stopped and put the menu slowly down. "Haiku Stairway," he said slowly, his tone low and serious.

"What's Haiku Stairway?" Arch asked, when Matisse failed to supply anymore.

"It's called the Stairway to Heaven, but it's not. It's the Stairway to Hell," Matisse answered, as he slid his eyes over to look at Arch's damaged hand.

X

Stairway to Heaven?" Arch said, looking intently into Matisse's eyes.

"I don't like the way you said that. What heaven or what hell are you talking about and what does it have to do with the word Haiku DeWare mentioned?"

Matisse waved the waitress away when she approached. "There's a metal stairway built during WWII up to the highest peak of the Koolau range. Over two thousand rungs going up as many feet. The rusted remains of those metal stairs remain to this day. People have died trying to climb them. Something about them involved in all this?"

"Oh," Arch replied. "I don't know, but there must be. What else could the word refer to? Where are the stairs?"

"Haiku," Matisse responded. "The steps start where H3 comes through the mountains on the windward side just up from Haiku Plantations and Gardens. There's a graveyard there that leads to path under the freeway and up to the base of the mountains. With your hand we can't even think about what you're thinking right now."

Arch held his hand in front of him, splayed as flat as he could make it on the tabletop. The wound no longer caused him agonizing pain, only a dull sort of throbbing ache. He tried to flex his fingers but could only get them to curve a small bit before grimacing and opening his hand again. He thought about the valley where the stairway base had to be. Near or possibly the same valley where it had all begun. Somehow he and Matisse were going to end up back down in that valley. The thought was anything but pleasant.

"We don't know anything for sure," Arch said, knowing he wouldn't be climbing any two thousand-rung ladders anytime soon, if ever. "We've got to find out more and I can see only one way since our assault on Bellows was such a blatant failure."

"Blatant?" Matisse inquired, waving the waitress over.

"Apparent, obvious, right in front of our faces," Arch replied, his tone acidic.

"How we get more to know?" Matisse asked before whispering some order to the waitress who bent down to hear him. He looked up into Arch's eyes when he was done ordering and his facial expression changed.

"Virginia the bitch," he whispered, almost sub vocally.

"What else can we do?" Arch said. "We're at a dead end. Bellows is closed off and we can't exactly go exploring the valley and climbing thousands of feet in the air without finding out what's going on. The big plane is only a clue. There's something bigger. Your own people are going to be wiped out or sent off to Guantanamo or some place like that for a long time unless we figure this out."

"How you know the bitch doesn't know?" Matisse responded.

"Don't call her that anymore," Arch ordered

"Okay, brah, but you know what I mean. Where we going find the Haole white cold woman?"

"North Shore," Arch answered, ignoring Matisse's sarcasm. "She's taken a vacation rental at Sunset Beach on one of those small back roads that parallel Kam Highway. Spending a pretty penny for luxury junk the Agency has not one clue about, I'm certain."

"Never done that sort of thing yourself, huh," Matisse said, not putting it out as a question.

"That's how I know," Arch shot back, absently, watching Matisse wolf down kabobs of teri steak and pork rib meat. Drinks were a fortune at the Moana, or at any of the hotels along the Waikiki shore except the

Sheraton, and food was even more. Arch didn't even what kind of balance he had left on his credit card. In the old days he'd have carried an Agency American Express made out to some phony company with no employees, no real address and no assets but unlimited credit. He waved at the waitress more to put a stopper in the eating and drinking open hole of Matisse's. Virginia wouldn't return to the house for anything but sleeping if she kept true to her workaholic "sleep only when absolutely required" regimen.

"Can't you call her and make an appointment over here on this side? It's an hour and a half across the Pali to Sunset. My friend Ahi is a Kuhuna over there though so maybe we can picnic in the park with him. Did you know that a man can walk across the sandy bottom of the bay offshore of Ahi's land and climb up on Chinaman's Hat at low tide?" Matisse finished his pile of meat and began licking his fingers.

"Not calling her," Arch concluded, doubting Matisse's comment about the offshore island simply because the tidal differentials weren't that great on any of the Hawaiian Islands, except maybe in Hilo Bay on the Big Island. "They'll just locate us using the phone. We need some throwaway phones from an ABC store. We're going to encounter her and get some details so we can help her and your people too. Unless you have something way better than threats to offer the Agency will find a home for your people somewhere in the middle of deepest darkest Africa."

"ABC's all over," Matisse complained. "Koreans run them all. Like Kim chi disease, or something. Samoan's took over the limo business and Tonga has a lock on security, which leaves singing and dancing for tips to real Hawaiians."

"You sing and dance?" Arch asked, starting to get a little bored by Matisse's never-ending comments about the Hawaiian Islands being taken from real Hawaiians by absolutely everyone else.

"Of course I sing and dance. I'm Kamaina!" Matisse answered, vehemently. He looked around the open patio bar as if to search out a ukulele or microphone.

Arch signed a credit card slip for somewhere over a hundred dollars including a minimal tip. "Let's go. Ahi's park is better than sitting around here being watched. I wish we had the Lincoln though, as your means of transportation is a little ostentatious."

"It's my car. I call her the Grappler. She always starts; always runs and I never have to change the oil. I got that synthetic stuff running in her guts." Matisse smiled hugely as they headed for the lobby of the hotel, his love of his ridiculous automobile beyond Arch's ability to comprehend.

They stopped at the ABC store on Kalakau long enough for Arch to run in and pick up a couple of forty dollar phones that should have been twenty. After Matisse's comment about never changing the oil in the Bonneville he wondered if they'd even make it over the mountains much less all the way into Sunset.

The trip out to the Pali was only exciting because of the way Matisse drove. For some reason he never got pulled over yet never drove close to the speed limit. They raced up the road to the Pali lookout. Just before they go to the Pali tunnel through the mountains Matisse jerked the wheel toward the right and they exited onto a narrow asphalt road. Arch saw a sign with "Scenic Highway" fly by. Suddenly, the car was traveling along a corridor totally covered by great splayed out trees. A tunnel of winding green foliage guided the fast-traveling car ever upwards until they reached a sharp turn suddenly ending at the beginning of a small parking lot. Matisse finally slowed, gently easing the convertible into a handicapped slot near the top edge of the lot. A local security guard, obviously Hawaiian, waved and smiled.

"My brah, from my sister's side," Matisse laughed, slamming the Bonneville's heavy car door with some gusto.

"Does he sing and dance too or, is that part of his day job," Arch asked with a wiry smile behind the other man's back. Matisse didn't answer, as they walked past the guard and on up to a hand built series of retaining walls. Tourists singly and in groups mulled about trying to hang onto skirts, cameras and bags in the ever-increasing wind. When they arrived at the shoulder-high wall itself Arch estimated the wind coming up over the edge to be traveling at nearly forty miles an hour.

"What are we doing here?" Arch finally asked Matisse, ducking back to be heard.

Matisse stood with his back to the wall instead of looking out over the edge at the gorgeous view of almost the whole windward side of the island.

"Take a look," Matisse answered, first pointing up toward a high peak beyond and above them. Then he turned and swept his pointing finger down toward an area just below and to the left of the bottom of the great cliff the Pali rose up to become the top of.

Arch stared whit his upturned at the imposing very high point of the peak and then let his eyes slide down toward the back of the cemetery toward where Matisse's finger remained pointing. A small valley seemed to run back from the cemetery and up into the seemingly solid rock of the Koolau range wall

"Haiku," Matisse said, his voice raised but still difficult to hear against the heavy wind.

"You've got to be kidding me," Arch breathed. "I sure hope our Haiku means something else entirely," he said more loudly. Matisse just grinned, and then turned and walked back to the Pontiac. "You afraid of heights, Haole?" he said without turning, the wind dying as they walked away from the edge of the Pali overlook. They drove in near silence the long twisting route of windward-side Kam Highway.

Ahi turned out to be an aging Hawaiian of huge girth. His identity and size had become apparent at the same time as the Pontiac stopped near the end of Chinaman's Hat Park an hour later. The early afternoon sun was blazing. Ahi's presence was even bigger than might otherwise be evident simply because he was standing on a small platform while a whole crowd of others were kneeling inside the open rolled up walls of a great outdoor tent.

"Ahi," Matisse stated, needlessly waiving one arm toward the tent.

"Why's everyone else kneeling?" Arch asked, walking toward the crowd at Matisse's side.

"Sunday," Matisse said, stopping outside the tent. "Ahi's talking chief, chief, father, preacher and my uncle on this side of the island. He's doing the Sunday service."

Arch wondered who wasn't related to Matisse on Oahu, in some weird way or other, and why the man knew almost every local but none seemed to care for him very much.

"We wait," Matisse stated, squatting down on the grass.

"Great," Arch replied, trying not to seem impatient but also glad for an opportunity to rest and bask in the sun. His hand hurt and his head felt like he was rolling around ideas and events so fast and without real purpose that he might be going crazy. They waited a full hour for Ahi to finish with his followers. The tent emptied and the people dispersed without comment, seeming not to notice the two indolent men waiting near one open wall.

Introductions were short, with Matisse simply remarking that Arch was his friend and that both of them would be trying to get into a house at Sunset Beach to talk to a Haole woman.

"Take some of my warriors," Ahi said, after listening to Matisse's introduction and what they were up to.

"Of course," Matisse responded, before Arch could say no.

The last thing Arch wanted was a bunch of amateur islanders mucking about and listening in on what was a very highly classified governmental program. He bit his lip but did nothing other than nod assent to his companion's verbal assent.

"So you talking chief for government or something like that?" Ahi asked, clasping his hands tightly across his significant chest.

Arch glanced at Matisse who averted his eyes. "Seems you know a bit about what I'm trying to do," he replied, realizing that he liked the big man lot for no reason whatever, which was a bit disconcerting. There was a warmth to his eyes and depth to his facial features Arch had only seen in older Native American men years ago in New Mexico.

"You do good for the people and we do good for you," the aging man of wisdom stated, as if talking to a disciple, but then a smile came to his face and Arch felt like they were almost friends.

They talked back and forth for nearly an hour, about the history of the Hawaiian people, the island of Oahu and even the strange homologated form of the mix of native and Catholic beliefs melded together to form the religion Ahi and his flock followed. Ahi was called away by some of the returning followers who needed his assistance in building an afternoon Luau. Matisse and Arch wandered down toward the point facing directly toward Medicine Hat Island. A small beach nuzzled into the lee side of the point, with a just enough room for only a very few people.

"So you want to hike out to the island?" Arch offered, as both men took sitting positions on two big rocks just back from the sand. Three-foot swells broke on the other side of the point while the swells moving straight toward the more distant bay beach expanse seemed rough and intimidating.

"Nah, tide's not right," Matisse replied, weakly, the water in front of them appearing a good deal deeper than any man or woman could stand in and still touch bottom.

"Who are these warriors Ahi's intent on supplying us with?" Arch asked.

"Not real people," Matisse replied. "That was his way of saying that we could go and do whatever we want to do to the bitch on his grounds…I mean that Haole woman," he modified quickly.

"Oh," was all Arch could say, his tone one of complete relief however.

"Ahi understand more than you think," Matisse offered.

"Gee, I wonder why that is?" Arch came back, neither expecting nor receiving a response.

The afternoon went quickly, the sun beginning to draw down toward the ocean horizon in the way it did to give a place like Sunset Beach its name. The Luau was replete with more Hawaiian foods than Arch had seen in one place since his early years on the island. By the time the sun was close to setting Arch wished he'd not partaken of so much of it.

"We go," Matisse said, tapping him on one shoulder. "We have Ahi's blessing, we need no more."

Arch grimaced but turned to follow his one apparent friend on all of Oahu, knowing that whatever Ahi claimed to possess in power over his lands and people both he and they were totally dominated by whatever the U.S. government chose to decide at any given time.

The Sunset Beach house wasn't difficult to find. A bronze and brass automatic beach gate ran the full length of its property. Beyond that a triple garage door was closed behind it. Video cameras protruded from both corners of the house. Security was high but Arch had expected that. Beach houses all shared one serious security weakness however and that was the beach itself. Whatever was put between the house and the beach decreased the value of the beach property. Some private owners along the North Shore built places of such security, walled from the very beach that was supposedly what attracted them to build there in the first place. Most builders however, particularly the ones that wanted to rent out their houses at exorbitant rates, took as much open advantage of their little stretches of beach as possible. Virginia's house was no exception to that rule which became readily apparent, as Matisse and Arch hiked first up to Sunset Beach itself and then back down toward the house. Only a single huge berm of sand stood out from the place, with palm trees and hedges defining the limits of that berm, that were no doubt placed right on top of property lines.

Arch crawled up to the end of one of the hedges and peered through the branches, like a spy in a cheap movie. He didn't expect to see anything or anyone, even though the sliding double door running half way across the back of the house gaped open. The wind blew the drapes out and wafted them back and forth over the lanai like huge bat wings. Two men walked into view, each man carrying an obvious cocktail in one hand. The men were easily identifiable as Kurt and Lorrie.

Arch reared back quickly, jamming his shoulder into Matisse's face. Matisse let out a loud groan. Arch and Matisse looked at one another, and then turned as one and began to run for cover sticking as close as they could to any cover toward Sunset Beach.

XI

Arch and Matisse hiked the quarter mile back past Sunset Beach until they came to Ted's Bakery. Ted Nakamura ran the place and he knew Matisse from way back, or so Matisse claimed. Ted wasn't there when they arrived and the place was packed. Some tourists, but mostly local surfers and other semi-rejects hung about inside the single small room or sprawled at rusting metal tables on the outside. Ted had expanded the outdoor eating to the other side of the parking lot, but no one ever went to sit at those tables, even just to wait for their orders. Arch read a sign on the cash register that said the credit card machine was broken. Matisse informed him that the machine had been broken since the nineties.

"You got cash?" Matisse whispered, between flirting exchanges he was making with the tired and beaten-looking women behind the counter.

"No, all I've got is my card," Arch responded, not really caring because he wasn't hungry anyway. The encounter at the beach house had involved running down the beach before Kurt and Lorrie could figure out they were there. Just one more element of demeaning abuse he'd suffered since arriving on Oahu only days earlier.

"No problem, brah, they got ATM," Matisse stuck out his hand.

Arch saw the ATM in the corner, sitting up next to a coffee machine, both looked barely functional. Cups sat next to the coffee machine, so he poured himself one before stepping in front of the ATM. "Seven dollars?" he hissed at the screen. He had no choice. The card was good for at least a hundred more dollars because bills started slipping one by one into a slot near Arch's right knee. Arch counted the money before realizing the old food-stained robot hadn't spit his card back out. He whacked the machine loudly with the flat palm side of his one good hand.

"Hey," Matisse interrupted. "This my friend," he said, pushing Arch aside. He put both his plate-sized hands against the sides of the machine and then leaned forward. He blew into the thin dirty slot Arch had put his card into. The machine gurgled with seeming glee before noisily spitting Arch's card out. Matisse put the card in his pocket, but Arch was right there with one hand extended when Matisse turned back to the counter to order.

"Are these more of the friends you don't have?" Arch asked, putting the card carefully into his wallet.

"I'll be across the tarmac in the other area," he said, handing over two twenties to Matisse. "I'm not hungry. But get whatever you need."

After only a few minutes, Matisse joined him at one of the empty tables. "They come get me. You got teri-plate with double mac and white rice. Give you energy. This best loco moco on windward side." Matisse put the remaining twenty on the table in front of Arch, sensing his dark mood.

"What now, brah?" Matisse asked.

"What now?" Arch questioned, looking up at the blowing palm reeds not far overhead. He looked back down. Only a few feet away, distant cars sped past on Kam Highway, while an old oriental man wearing only one rubber "go-ahead" slipper tried to work his arm down into a rusty container containing used soft drink cans. For some reason chicken wire mesh had been placed over the top of the can. This allowed the man's arm to reach in and grab cans, but wouldn't let him pull his arm back out with a can still in it. The old man continued to struggle without sound or comment, but couldn't seem to extricate his arm, and wouldn't let go of a can to help himself.

"Christ!" Arch said, his voice an exasperated hiss. He got up and walked over to the struggling man. With one foot he struck the side of the old oil barrel with all his strength. As both the barrel and the old man fell to the ground, the top broke loose from the impact. The old man sat up and worked his arm slowly back out of the mesh, and then began collecting the cans that spewed forth. Without acknowledging Arch in any way, he placed several cans carefully into his old backpack, slung it over his shoulder, and then walked carefully away on the very edge of the road, his one thong making a smacking sound every time it hit the asphalt.

Arch watched the bent old man re-adjust his load from time to time until he disappeared. He made his way back to Matisse's side, but stopped just before he got there.

"That's it," he said, his expression changing from wrinkled depression to smiling delight. "We kick the stupid can. We've been caught, beaten, tortured, abused and then caught again. But we've got a gun, and guns are something I'm really good at. Let's go kick the can and see what comes rolling out."

One of the used up looking women from the bakery appeared, her arms laden with paper plates. Arch sat next to Matisse, trying to curb his new enthusiasm. All of a sudden the teri-plate the woman set down in front of him looked delightful, as did the plate set in front of Matisse. After unloading a small bag of condiments and plastic silverware, the woman removed her last package. It was obviously a pie box. When she put the box down she said "Chocolate Hupia Pie from Ted," and departed.

Arch took one bite of the macaroni salad and then proceeded to eat both scoops without stopping. The macaroni salad at Ted's was legendary and it was obvious why. He watched Matisse go to work on his huge Loco Moco. Prime rib gravy flowed down the sides of his mouth, as he downed half the giant burger patty laying atop three fried eggs and a mound of sticky white rice the gravy flowed around. When Arch was done with his teri-plate he walked over to the bakery's main building and used the bathroom. On his way back he thought about the pie and what the word Haupia might mean. Matisse sat contentedly back in his seat waiting for him, sipping from a can of Guava soda.

"How's the pie?" Arch asked leaning down to open the box.

"Oh," was all Matisse said, just before Arch saw that the box was empty.

"The whole pie?" Arch asked. "You ate the whole damned pie? Nobody can eat a whole pie in only a few seconds."

"Ah, maybe you were gone longer than you thought," Matisse answered, getting up to put their used plates into a nearby trashcan.

"You gotta have some of that Haupia pie soon, brah," he murmured when he came back.

They walked together back to where the Pontiac was parked. Arch thought it was appropriate that no other vehicle ever seemed to park very close to the bizarre looking car. "What's haupia mean?" He asked Matisse, who was gingerly leaning against the Bonneville's hood.

"Coconut," Matisse responded. "Coconut cream, if you mean in Ted's pie." He looked over at Arch. "What's next?"

"You don't have to come," Arch said. "I'm taking the gun and going right back at them through the double door. Somebody's likely to get shot, and probably I'll be that person. You can wait here and see what happens. I'm done being a punching bag for this outfit. They're up to their necks in something that's dark and deadly dangerous to a lot of people. And I'm not quitting until I know what it is."

"Why?" Matisse asked. They were both silent for a moment, watching tourists gather to go down into the knee-high waves below. "You retired. Why go on? You can go fishing or travel or do something else with your life."

"Like what?" Arch shot back, instantly. "I've traveled. I don't like fishing. You and Virginia are about the only friends I've been able to make. I'm not doing very well with her and I've only known you for how many days?"

"Okay, but going in there and shooting everyone if they don't, won't or can't talk seems dumb. Ahi does have some guys. Why don't we go back and see him. Maybe if a bunch of the people show up with us nobody has to get shot. The people were up against aren't like that drunk getting old soda cans out of the trash."

"So, you're not coming with me?" Arch said.

"No, I'll go," Matisse answered immediately. After a few seconds he added: "I just think we should talk to Ahi first. He's been on this side of Oahu longer than we've been alive. Maybe he knows something that can help. If we shoot those men, or even Virginia, they'll lock us up at Halawa for a lot of years."

"I'm not going to shoot Virginia," Arch said. His tone was softer, his words coming out slower and more contemplative.

"Not on purpose. Once shooting starts though, anything can happen," Matisse said.

Arch looked over at his newfound friend in surprise. The rough -talking, hard-eating islander was taking an unexpected tack. "We've got time. Okay, it's only half an hour back, but my mind's pretty much made up."

"Nah," Matisse replied, pointing back the way they'd driven in from.

"Ahi at Kahuku this hour on Sunday. His wife works shift at Kahuku Hospital only seven miles. Five minutes, maybe less without traffic."

The ridiculous Pontiac, which hadn't had an oil change for God knew how many miles, turned over and started instantly with a gutty roar. Matisse always pumped the accelerator for half a minute before turning on the ignition, no matter how many times Arch told him he was flooding the carburetor. Matisse drove the seven miles at his usual dangerous clip, passing cars in no passing zones and waving at almost all pick up trucks they came across, moving or stopped. It didn't seem to matter if anyone was in the parked trucks, Arch noted.

Matisse parked in a doctor's parking spot at the very front of the hospital. They got out and went inside the emergency entrance. Matisse seemed to know every nook and cranny of the place as they made their way through the labyrinth of the complex. He said "hey" to everyone they passed, or simply made the Shaka symbol, which involved extending the index and little fingers of his right hand while wiggling his wrist. They found Ahi holding court at the back corner of the cafeteria, once more surrounded by a group of local people sitting instead of kneeling. Matisse stopped Arch from approaching by putting out his meaty left hand and hitting him on the chest.

"He's talking story," Matisse observed. "We wait for break. He's seen us so it'll only be a little bit. Let's have some fried chicken. It's great here. Coffee over there. Molokai Peaberry. Da best. Free. Two bucks really, but nobody ever says anything if you don't pay."

Arch got a cup of coffee and gave his card to the cashier, indicating that she should put Matisse's heaping plate of chicken on the bill. The woman smiled a big smile and put the questionable card on the lip of her register.

Matisse joined him a few minutes later. "Signed for the stuff, hope that's okay," he said, plopping Arch's card on the table between them.

He began working his way through the chicken, pushing a drumstick over in front of Arch. Arch looked down at the overly blackened thing but took a single bite anyway. Like almost all food cooked by locals in Hawaii, it was unbelievably delicious. He took small bites until only the bone was left. Ahi stood, as Arch was finishing, and wading through his little group of followers, and made his way ponderously to their table.

"Permission to sit?" he asked, unexpectedly.

"Sure," Arch said, puzzled by the man's strange use of words

Ahi smiled broadly. "I was a Marine, so many years back." He turned the end chair around and sat down on it, cradling his huge forearms over the back.

Arch didn't know what to say, he was so surprised.

"You got trouble because the meeting at the house didn't go so well?" the big Hawaiian asked.

"No," Arch answered, truthfully. "It didn't go at all. Virginia might be there or she may not. The guy who did this to my hand was there, with his partner, both armed. I wanted to go in but Matisse said we needed to talk to you first. So here we are."

"The Marine Corps' frontal assault' not always bad, but usually only works with a lot of casualties." Ahi said the words with a smile, his dark eyes seeming to twinkle.

"Yeah, that's what Matisse said," Arch replied, glancing over at Matisse who was working his way through an entire fried chicken not long after consuming a monster breakfast and a whole pie. "What do you think?" Arch asked, finally.

"They got a big plane at Bellows," Ahi said. "Landed in the night some time back. Lots of wind from that plane. What's on it is important. Somehow it's connected very deeply with something in the mountains here. And this is my land, my people's land."

Arch was surprised again. It had taken Arch days to find out the same information, and not nearly in as much detail as Ahi had.

"There's a woman named Virginia in charge of the operation, only not really," Arch said. "General DeWare from Kaneohe seems to be her boss, although I'm not sure of anything there. She's at that house on Sunset. I need to talk to her about everything, and I can't do that if she's guarded by some armed men. Matisse thinks it's a bad idea to use the frontal assault, so again, here we are. Any suggestions?"

"John Martin," Ahi said, after almost a full minute of staring up at the foam ceiling of the cafeteria.

"John Martin?" Arch asked, baffled.

"Actually, Sergeant John Martin," Ahi replied, his eyes coming back down to meet Arch's own. "He runs the Honolulu P.D. over here. Got put out to pasture years ago for drunk driving. Now he's the man."

"Haole man, like me, running the police over here?" Arch asked, in surprise again.

"You not Haole," Ahi laughed. "You here so long you like one of the people. You Kamaaina. And John has a Haole name, but he actually one of the people. Ohana. Of the land."

Arch accepted the huge compliment with a big smile of his own. The "H"-word was almost universally used by locals to describe Caucasians in Hawaii, whether they were born there generations ago or simply visiting as a tourist, and generally they used it right to their faces. "So, what's Sergeant Martin supposed to be able to do here?"

"John brings a bunch of the guys in uniform," Ahi said. "What can they do? Shoot the police? Arrest them? I don't think so. You get Virginia's attention. Maybe no violence. I'll come too. I've been shot before."

"Shot before? Marines?" Arch asked.

"The Nam. An Hoa. Sixty-Nine." Ahi answered, his expression turned deadpan serious.

"You don't look that old," Arch said, with doubt in his voice.

"You don't look like a spy. You don't look like a tough man. You don't look like you're violent. You don't look lost or like you don't have a life. You don't look like you're old enough either. Some of us have that ability, not to look like what we are or what we should look like from where we've been."

Arch absorbed what the big Hawaiian said without speaking for a moment. Matisse finished his chicken, then licked his fingers clean before using several napkins. Arch thought he detected a vague knowing smile on the man's lips while he worked.

"John Martin and his merry men it is," Arch said, finally.

"We go Laie Point?" Matisse asked, getting to his feet.

"I'll call. Take a few minutes for John to gather his guys together," Ahi responded. He took out a new iPhone 6 from a hip pocket with some difficulty, before standing and backing away from the table.

Matisse smiled and followed Ahi but only to dump his tray of trash into a nearby bin. He returned to once again sit across from Arch. "See, I told you. What can they do at that house if we show up with a bunch of local cops? Ahi's the man. My brah."

"Really? What happens when those clowns inside the house simply fail to come to the door and there we all stand in the driveway?" Arch replied, slowly shaking his head. "They'll know we know where the house is too."

Ahi pocketed his phone and walked to the edge of the table. "They're coming. John was a Marine too. He loves this kind of stuff. I don't know how many of his buddies are coming but it should be enough."

They walked back through the convoluted corridors of the hospital until they arrived out by the car.

"I'll put the top down," Matisse volunteered. Arch wondered if Ahi would fit into the cavernous back seat even with the top down. It took a few minutes, and not a little effort, to get loaded into the car, but then they were on the road. Matisse took the car up to blinding speed, closing fast on some tourist's rental car in front of them. Ahi leaned forward and briefly gripped Matisse's shoulder before letting go. Matisse immediately slowed the Pontiac and followed the tourist Toyota all the way back to Sunset Beach. Arch would have thanked Ahi but the passing wind in the convertible was too loud for his voice to he heard.

The turn down onto the access road unexpectedly became dramatic, as they approached the outer gate normally blocking entry to the house. Two unmarked vans and a bunch of privately owned police cars clogged the entire area. The gate to the house and the garage door were gaping open. Several officers were standing at the back of a black Chevy Suburban parked inside the garage. Matisse pulled the Pontiac up close to the back of one of the vans and shut it down. Both men helped Ahi extricate himself from the rear seat. The officers stopped talking and watched them approach.

"Inside," one uniformed officer said, pointing toward the wall at the back of the garage.

Arch was the first one through the back door. He passed through a short corridor and then into the residence's ground floor main room. The big double glass door gaped open, as it had before, with the drapes still flapping in the light wind. Virginia sat on a long couch facing him, her eyes hugely round, her mouth sealed shut with a piece of duct tape. Duct tape also held her knees together, and it was obvious that something held her arms together behind her back. A tall, dark and handsome police officer stood next to Virginia's right shoulder. He was in uncommonly good physical condition without an ounce of fat, much less the usual thick layer most islanders carried around.

"Ahi, uncle!" the officer exclaimed, as Ahi trundled in with Matisse just before him. "You said the woman shouldn't speak until you got here so this is the only way we could shut her up. The fellas she was with are upstairs, a little less comfortable, but okay. I put their guns in the trash compactor. All you have to do is push the button. We also restrained them with tape so you don't need keys or any of that. Anything else?"

"You want to know what this is about?" Ahi asked his nephew.

"Nah, uncle, they not very interesting. No drugs, just a lot of talk about how important they are. Call us if you need anything." Several other officers in SWAT uniforms began to file down the stairs. In seconds the house was nearly empty.

Arch sat next to Virginia on the couch and began to slowly peel the duct tape from her face whispering "I'm so sorry" as he worked.

XII

Peeling the duct tape from Virginia's face was like peeling skin from the surface of a Kiwi fruit. Virginia said nothing. Her eyes spoke for her and there was as much warmth in them as there is warmth emanating from the bottom of blue glacier ice.

"There," Arch announced, with a tepid smile and a small forced laugh.

Then he went to work on freeing her bound wrists. Matisse handed over a small pocketknife, with the blade exposed, to assist. Being very careful not to injure the woman further, Arch sliced slowly through the sticky tape.

"You bastard," Virginia breathed out, using the fingers of both freed hands to massage and smooth the lower part of her face. "I see you've added some more fat to your ridiculous band of local swine," she continued, glaring first at Matisse and then Ahi, both standing on the other side of the small coffee table that separated them.

"Where's the Haole woman?" Ahi asked, craning his huge head to look around the room. "Where's the, you know, the wonderful Haole woman you love?"

Matisse turned his head to avoid the appearance of laughing openly.

Arch frowned at the Abbot and Costello routine he was observing, but his attention was caught by the faint sound of someone using the front stairs.

"Who's in the house?" he asked, thinking of Kurt and Lorrie left bound and gagged upstairs by John Martin's hastily gathered team of whatever they were. Neither Matisse nor Ahi made any response.

"I want you and your flock of Kanaka lemmings to get the hell out of my house right now," Virginia ordered. In emphasis, she rose unsteadily to her feet while pointing toward the glass double doors still gaping open in the wind. As all eyes in the room turned to look where she was pointing, a man walked through the curtains.

"No one seems to be answering the front door," General DeWare said, entering and stopping when he was a few feet from Matisse's right shoulder.

"Apparently, that didn't deter you," Arch responded, putting the General's sudden appearance together with the footsteps he'd heard earlier.

"I presume the two imbeciles you have working for you are running free to commit more stupidity?"

"Enough with the verbal jousting," DeWare answered, raising one hand as if to ward off further comments. "I think it's time we all had a talk about what's going on and what needs to be done,"

"Now why don't I think that's going to happen?" Arch asked, rising to his feet and standing next to Virginia.

"This isn't a secure place," the general said, acting like Arch hadn't even spoken. "Let's all meet in half an hour at the Haleiwa Café. There won't be anyone there at this hour after lunch. No recordings. Nobody will be listening in. We can be frank with one another."

Arch marveled at the smooth delivery of the man and his obvious ability to immediately take and hold control of the situation. The knowledge made him dislike the man all the more. "Do you think we're that dumb? If you wanted listening devices then they'd already be in place. The Café is probably another of your little "safe house" operations." Arch knew he was sounding paranoid and possibly silly but he couldn't stop himself. The general seemed to garner all of Virginia's attention every time he was on the scene. Arch glanced at Virginia's face for any kind of support but she only had eyes for the general, her head nodding like one of those bobbing doll's to be found in the back window of some old classic car.

"Your rental's out front parked on the road," DeWare said, tossing the Lincoln's keys to Virginia instead of Arch. Arch snatched the keys in mid-air, only realizing afterward that the gesture revealed just how much the man was successfully playing on his angry emotion.

Arch tool a few deep breaths, slowly sliding the key fob into his right front pocket. "Okay, half an hour. The Café." Before he could add anything more Virginia walked over the general and they went out through the double doors together, leaving Arch standing with Matisse and Ahi in front of him.

"That went well," Ahi observed.

"He has troubled relationships," Matisse added in Arch's defense.

"Shut up. Both of you," Arch stated, flatly. "There are a lot more serious implications about all this. What's going on between Virginia and I is none of your business."

"Okay, and it's the first time any of them, anyone at all, has been willing to talk to us since this started," Ahi agreed.

"Matisse, check and see if those clowns upstairs are gone, "Arch ordered. "And both of you please remember that I'm not part of your cause, no matter what I believe about it. I came here because of the woman and got thrown into whatever this is, but I'm not siding with you guys or anybody else."

"You just called her 'the woman,'" Ahi replied.

"Will you stop with these inane observations?" Arch shot back.

Matisse returned to report that the two bound men were gone, as predicted. They all walked silently out to where the Pontiac was parked. The Lincoln was about a hundred feet further down the road. Arch noted that the afternoon sun was hotter than normal when a spot was occupied where the trade winds didn't reach.

"C'mon, we'll take the Lincoln. It has air," Arch said, walking toward the rental while clicking the locks open with his key fob.

"They had the Lincoln," Ahi said, using his understated 'Wisdom of Buddha' tone.

"They returned it," Matisse said, as the three approached the car together, "and it looks like they even washed it. Only the Marines would do that," he finished proudly.

"That's not what he meant," Arch said, stopping at the driver's door and looking into the cars interior. "We don't know much yet, and it might be valuable to some people if we didn't know anymore. Let's take the Bonneville. With the top down it'll be fine as long as it's not driven at a hundred miles an hour." Arch stared at Matisse meaningfully when he was done.

"A bomb? A bomb? Are we talking about a bomb?" Matisse, said, astonishment coloring his every word.

"Probably not anything so dramatic, or drawing as much attention. Probably just bugged to high heaven," Arch answered, turning to head back to where the Pontiac was parked.

Ahi took up most of the back seat while Arch drove shotgun. For the first time the Pontiac did not start instantly when Matisse turned the key.

"Oh no, my luck's run out. Please start," cajoled Matisse, lovingly patting the car's steering wheel with his spare hand as he used the other to turn the ignition key.

"Stop before you run down the battery," Arch instructed. "Pop the hood." Arch got out and walked to front of the car. He pulled up on the heavy hood. There was no secondary latch. "The distributor top is loose," he observed, leaning forward and down to snap the part back into place.

He dropped the hood when he was done, its slamming sound echoing back and forth off the ugly cinder block walls located on each side of the road.

Hawaii was a place of opposites and anachronisms. Intense living beauty interrupted everywhere with drop-dead ugliness. The trick was not to notice the ugliness and enjoy the beauty part.

The car started with its usual instant élan. Matisse lowered the electric powered top, which for unknown reasons still worked, and took off like he was leaving the Launchpad at Canaveral.

"That never happen before," he yelled over the growing buffet of the wind.

"Detached motivation," Arch answered. "One car doesn't start, you have a half an hour to make a half an hour trip so you use the other car available instead of mucking with the dead one. If they wanted to plant a bomb they'd have put it in this one without giving us another. And if they did what they obviously did, then we've probably got a few more surprises coming."

"Man, you evil thinking," Matisse, responded, laughing into the wind.

"No, he's just smart," Ahi said from the back seat, his voice barely audible over the noise of their passage.

It took twenty minutes to get to the outskirts of Haleiwa, mostly because the tourists blocked the road at Turtle Beach to cross and see the many animals there. The authorities had made it as difficult to pull over and screw up the traffic as possible, but their efforts made little or no difference. On the weekend, the wait was at least ten minutes just to get by the hundred-yard stretch of Kam Highway, without killing or maiming anyone. Matisse took the first turn off instead of using the bypass to come at the town from the other side. The Haleiwa Café was near the far end of the town.

When the car was slowed to five miles an hour by the downtown traffic on the narrow two-lane shop covered road, it became quiet enough inside the car to be heard.

"I love driving through town," Matisse pointed out. "We got plenty time. People love my car. They all smile and wave."

"Yeah, all your great local friends," Arch said, acidly.

"Many people love Makaha, Matisse, but they have difficulty showing true affection," Ahi concluded.

As the car went past the partially closed Matsumoto Shave Ice General Store, an unmarked gray van pulled out from the side of the road into the side of the Pontiac. The van caromed away, and then took an immediate right down into Longs Drug Store parking lot. Matisse jerked the wheel to keep from having a head on accident with an oncoming truck.

"Pakatadi," Matisse yelled, using an virulent Japanese epithet.

He steered the Pontiac to the side of the road and stopped, with Arch leaning into his right shoulder, having barely avoided his arm being ripped off from the van's impact. He cradled his damaged hand against his stomach.

"You okay, Ahi?" Matisse inquired, looking back.

"It seems your friend was correct," Ahi said, seemingly unhurt and unmoved by the crash.

Matisse accelerated the Bonneville back into the traffic but turned right down into the Long's lot. The van had been held up in traffic. They all saw its taillights blink red as it turned into the loading alley behind the local drug store. Matisse blasted the Pontiac forward, ignoring tourists jumping away on foot, and seemingly oblivious to the many moving cars in the lot. He pulled past the alley and stopped the car violently, driving them all forward inside the passenger compartment.

"For Christ's sake Matisse, what in hell are you doing?" Arch complained, his hand once again painfully jostled.

"I see the bastard," Matisse answered. "He's sitting at the end of the alley. He's blocked by the dumpster. Got him. Nobody does that to my Bonny! Nobody! I show them some demolition derby driving trick. You hit them with back of car, not front or side. Then you can keep driving. Ha ha!"

Matisse gunned the Pontiac and threw it into reverse. He pulled into the alley, one arm swung over the seat, his neck craning around and accelerated the Bonneville. With both Arch and Ahi yelling "no" at the same time the car flew backwards and straight into the rear of the van. Arch and Ahi had time to duck down and allow the seats to take the full force of the impact. The van flew up, sideways and then into a nearby palm tree. Matisse pulled the Pontiac a few feet forward.

"Now we mash 'em into pulp," he cried vengefully.

"Stop," Arch commanded, grabbing the steering wheel with his good hand.

Kurt's head appeared above the lip of the driver's side window on the van. His fingers clutched over the open window's edge. He stared with huge eyes at the Pontiac's twisted rear end.

"Enough," Ahi commanded Matisse, joining Arch in trying to stop the man's obvious rage.

"Fine. Just fine," Matisse said, in a forceful but pouting tone. They wreck my car and that's it. I'm tired of everybody wrecking me and all my stuff and getting away with it."

Arch took his hand from the wheel and patted Matisse softly on the shoulder. "You're right. None of this is your fault. I am your friend, and I want to thank you for all you've done."

"Really?" Matisse asked, in surprise. "Really?"

"The van was to destabilize us, not to hurt us, at least not to hurt us much. Let's go. You think the car can make it, we've only got a couple of minutes and those bastards will probably leave if we're not on time. This whole routine is called "take the pebbles from my hand."

Matisse eased the car forward experimentally. "She'll do. Tough car my Pontiac, but somebody's going to pay to make her look like Queen Emma again." He moved the vehicle gingerly through the Long's lot and back into the Haleiwa traffic. "What pebbles?" he asked, finally.

"There was an old television show about a bunch of monks who were specialists in the martial arts. Every weekly show would open with a young acolyte being asked to try to grab three stone pebbles from a highly trained monk's open hand. The acolyte could never grab them in time before the monk closed his hand. The opening segment always had the monk holding out his hand and saying "take the pebbles from my hand."

"Okay," Matisse said, as they approached the end of Haleiwa and the café, "but what does it mean to us?"

"It means that these people are trying to force us to be the acolytes, while they are the trained wise old monks," Ahi answered. "It's about psychology."

"It also means they want something from us or they wouldn't bother," Arch added.

The run down café sat facing the road. It had an old western saloon-style front door, and a front portico that was nearly falling apart with wood rot, termite damage and decay. Matisse pulled alongside the building and drove down the thin dusty white alley to the parking lot in the rear. The dust wasn't from gravel or dirt. It was from dried old reef material that'd been ground up and then spread to cover the dirt. There was little doubt that the general was inside the restaurant with plenty of reinforcement. Government-style black Chevy Suburbans, and even a thinly disguised Marine Corps staff car, were parked illegally on the grass of an adjoining empty lot.

"This place remains the dump it's always been," Arch commented, getting out the car.

"Maybe," Matisse responded, "but it's run by my friends."

"Of course, what a shock." Arch said, shaking his head wearily, while leading them to the crummy building's front door.

Arch opened the ratty torn screen door, and stepped into a different world.

The general and Virginia sat at their own table in the middle of the single room. The room was about the size of regular master bedroom in a tract home. The tables around the room were occupied by men and women who gave every appearance of being military, but were dressed like the general, in local Aloha attire. There wasn't one male, of the fifteen in the room, who had hair more than an inch long. The other distinctive feature of the place was the obvious addition of white tablecloths on all the tables.

Nobody in the place moved or said a word except for the general. He stood up and greeted them with a smile. "Table for five, just as agreed," DeWare said, expansively holding out an open hand toward them with his palm facing up.

"Take the pebbles from my hand," Matisse whispered almost silently from just behind Arch.

XIII

Arch took a seat next to Virginia, who acted like he wasn't there, staring at her upraised menu as if it offered something other than common island fare. Ahi and Matisse sat across from them with General DeWare holding court at one end.

"Did we really come in here to eat at this hour?" Arch asked Virginia, ignoring his own menu but allowing the waitress to pour him a cup of coffee. The waitress went on to fill all of their upturned cups without asking if anyone else wanted coffee. An ancient rock and roll song popular on Oahu in the sixties but heard almost nowhere else blared out softly from the kitchen: "Pearly shells, on the ocean, shining in the sun, covering up the shore…"

"So what's it going to be, more threats, or another attack by the two idiots we left bleeding back behind Longs Drugs?" Arch asked DeWare directly. Arch did not fail to note that Virginia hadn't distanced herself from his right elbow, which was barely touching her own atop the rather small table. He looked up to see Matisse smirking back at him. He eased his elbow away from Virginia's.

"This is a 'Q' clearance conversation, Mr. Patton," DeWare began, and you don't hold that level of clearance. In fact I don't think you ever held that level, and your two associates here have nothing at all."

"If you're going to ask them to leave then I'm leaving with them, no matter what you order your Gestapo agents to pull next," Arch replied, keeping his tone as unemotional as possible.

"Just tell them," Virginia said, putting her menu down in front of her.

"I can't tell you everything and besides it wouldn't be in your best interest to know everything anyway," DeWare replied. "Give us the room, " he said in his general's voice, turning to stare expressive around them.

The restaurant cleared quickly, the waitresses being escorted out by some of the fake customers. In less than a minute the place was empty.

"I've tried that before, but nobody left the room when I did," Arch observed, his tone one of humorous wry disdain.

"Perhaps, if you'd been a real general you might have had more success," DeWare replied without any humor at all.

"Okay, I can tell you this much, DeWare followed, his voice turning even more edged. "The plane at Bellows isn't going anywhere. It was meant to fly something in that couldn't have been brought in any other way. The pollution you've complained about is minimized and there will be no more of it. The escaped material would never register anything greater than a person might register receiving a couple of medical CAT scans. Virginia?"

"He's telling the truth," Virginia said, nodding while she said it. We need the power to drive the communication streams among different points on the islands. But that's it. That's all we can say, and that's probably too much. The plane needs to be left alone and any public interest in Bellows needs to go away."

"And Matisse and my people?" Ahi asked, his voice deep and serious.

"Not my department," DeWare replied immediately. "If they land at Bellows Beach they'll be taken into custody and spend the duration of mission years in administrative segregation. If they fire on anybody, then they'll die, all of them right out there on Rabbit Island."

The room went quiet. Arch watched DeWare and Virginia closely but said nothing.

"Well?" Virginia asked impatiently.

"Years? Islands? Communication streams?" Arch replied after a few seconds in complete surprise. "The mission is expected to last for years and it involves more than one island?" Arch stopped talking and stared at DeWare with a deep frown, not missing the fact that the general had steered very clear of mention the word radiation when he'd talked about pollution.

"Shit," DeWare stated tersely.

"Don't beat yourself up Horace, you're not trained for this kind of reading between the lines and he is," Virginia said, patting the general's left hand lightly with her right.

"Horace?" Arch and Matisse said at the same time.

"Do you call him 'Hor' for short?" Arch asked Virginia, smiling back at Matisse's gaping expression.

"And my people?" Ahi broke in, his words delivered in the same slow drumbeat cadence as before.

"What do you people want to get the hell out of here?" DeWare said, "All of you."

"There are eleven factions in the sovereignty movement," Ahi answered slowly, his tone changed to a lighter more analytical one as he talked. "The sisters at the university have money and land. Bumpy in Waimanalo has power for his faction. The other islands have Ohana, some land and even a bit of money. What do we get?"

"You expect the United States Marine Corps to write you a check? DeWare replied, angrily, "we're right back where we started with all this. We can, however, lock the three of you up right now and throw away the damned key."

"We're not exactly where we were," Arch replied. "We know a hell of a lot more, like how badly you don't need any of this to be in the media or all over Waikiki or even the other islands. You might lock me up, and even Matisse, but there's no way Ahi is going away without a whole lot of public and private trouble."

"You're lucky to get your lives, to keep your lives as you know them to be," DeWare shot back in a deadly tone. "We gave you as much as we can and if you don't like it you can go to hell."

"Three million dollars," Virginia said, into the momentary silence, her big black eyes locked into Ahi's own. They stared at one another while Matisse and Arch looked shocked and the general frowned to the point where his eyebrows met in the middle of his wrinkled forehead.

The table went silent again as Ahi considered the obvious offer.

"Land," Ahi stated, flatly, placing one of his pie plate-sized hands on the table between them.

"One block," Virginia replied, " about a quarter acre, on the edge of Kaneohe Marine Base near where that phony Earthtrust environmental outfit used to be."

"Bullshit," DeWare hissed at Virginia, "you can't give away military base property at your whim. That would take an act of Congress."

"Or a presidential order," Virginia replied, turning her face toward him with a pleasant-seeming cold smile.

"President?" Arch asked. "Other islands? Nuclear power plants flown in with unlikely leakage flowing out into the ocean? Communications of some weird higher order? What's going on here? This isn't any kind of mission I've ever heard of, much less been a part of. Next you'll be talking about interplanetary war and UFOs."

DeWare and Virginia stared at Arch, without comment following, until well past the end of his quietly delivered tirade.

"You're not an agent anymore, so you're out of it entirely," DeWare finally responded while Virginia went back to looking at her cheap torn menu.

"What do you want?" Virginia asked Arch, without taking her eyes away from the menu.

"I want to make sure you're safe and I want to know what's really going on," Arch answered, deliberately bumping her elbow to demand more engagement, "and I want you to tell me that there's no alien bullshit in any of this. That UFO reference was meant to be a joke." Arch said the words and waited. A cold feeling had become to form in the middle of his stomach when neither Virginia nor DeWare had batted an eye or taken his comment as being anything but serious.

"Can she do it?" Ahi asked into the silence.

"The Three million?" Arch answered with his own question. "Yes, if the president is playing on their team they can probably do whatever they want, assuming national security is somehow mixed into the bargain, or worse.

"I accept under one condition," Ahi agreed, "and that one's easy. I won't abandon my friends Matisse and Arch here since, having personal experience now, you people don't seem to mind committing almost any act of violence to accomplish your unknown mission of mystery."

"If everyone follows the agreement we make here then no more violence but if there is any violation, and I mean any violation, then anything may happen, and you don't have to abandon your friends, you simply have to stay away from them and out of it," DeWare stated, spreading his hands to either side, as if welcoming such an unspecified violation. "You agree, Virginia?" he added with a fake smile, his unblinking eyes never leaving Arch's.

Virginia looked at Arch before slowly nodding her head slowly.

Arch looked from DeWare to Virginia and back, still uncertain as to who was really in charge. Virginia's uncommon reticence and her obvious lack of willingness to approve across the board violence only strengthened his resolve.

"What about the Stairway to Heaven?" he asked of DeWare.

"Shit," DeWare hissed out again. "How in hell?"

"Enough!" Virginia cut in between the vitriolic looks passing between DeWare and Arch. "That's classified, and you damned well know it Arch.

Stop baiting him. Give in and get the hell out. I don't want or need your damaged, macho and entirely misplaced form of protection. You don't ever stop violence. Wherever you go and whatever you do violence follows you around like Pigpen's cloud."

"Me? Your people did this to my hand," Arch replied, his tone more hurt than angry. "Your people smashed their van into our car not twenty minutes ago half a mile from where we sit. I didn't do anything except come out here to see you. Instead I run into a weak-kneed substitute of a real Marine, and you put me back in play with a traitor for a partner and the two stooges acting like Keystone Cops trying to abuse me."

"You shot Lorrie in the hand, probably crippling him for life, and God only knows what shape their in back at Longs," Virginia replied, her tone icy cold and deliberate.

"We're done here," DeWare said, getting to his feet. "We've got a deal, if I can make the extortion thing happen with the land. You handle the money thing Virginia. I don't want to know anything about that. And as for you Corporal Patton, or whatever your real appropriate rank was, I hope you stick up your ugly macho head again. Next time you'll be at the other end of a Recon sniper's bullet. The only reason you're alive now is because I wouldn't let that Apache take you out."

"And there you go again," Arch replied, instantly, getting to his own feet. "Only the Army has Apache choppers and they don't take orders from Marines. None of any of this should be happening in the real world."

Suddenly, Virginia stood and turned. She hugged Arch to her, and whispered into his right ear. "I love you. I know you can't understand. Thank you for trying." She pushed herself away and took DeWare's hand in her own. "Tomorrow morning Mr. Ahi, the money will be delivered by cashier's check out to your hang-out near Chinaman's Hat. You can have your people set up shop in our vacated Earthtrust offices whenever you want."

DeWare and Virginia walked out the front door of the restaurant, leaving Ahi, Matisse and Arch at the table. Arch fell rather than sat back into his chair across form the two other men.

"Our vacated Earthtrust offices? It just keeps on not adding up. Earthtrust is or was CIA? How can that be? How awful is that?" he breathed the sentences out slowly, his mind roiling with all the disjointed pieces of a puzzle he couldn't quite grasp. Meanwhile, inside his heart twisted, watching Virginia lightly kiss DeWare on the café's lanai before they parted, and deep down he felt the first twinges of fear concerning what he'd gotten himself into. He knew he wasn't getting himself out of whatever it was until things made more sense.

"I am truly sorry Arch," Ahi began, looking down at this big hands lying flat on the table between them. "The money makes our cause. The land, however small, is to be our land and our starting place. Our movement is going from renting to ownership overnight."

"So you're out. I get it. I've used enough bribes in my career and I've never known a big enough one to be turned down. What about you, my new supposed friend," he said, directing his words to Matisse."

Matisse looked over at Ahi, who did not meet his eyes, before turning his attention back to Arch. "As you can see, I don't have many friends because none of my friends agree with me about anything. I'm stuck with you. The Stairway to Heaven. It's got to be the key. Did you see how angry that fake general got when you brought it up? We only know about the stairs because of me."

"He's the real general, and I'm the fake one, Matisse. But you're right about the stairway. There's something up there at the very top of the Koolaus and maybe it's the key. What are you going to do?"

"I'm going with my friend. But we have to go somewhere else first," he concluded, his face bright with enthusiasm and good humor.

"Where?" Arch replied, for some reason much more relieved than he thought he might be.

"Before the stairway we've got to go back down in that valley," Matisse grinned hugely. "Down in the valley of the shadow of death."

XIV

Matisse drove the Bonneville with less than his usual abandon. The Sunday afternoon traffic on Kam Highway was simply overwhelming and there was no place to pass, illegally or otherwise, along the entire length of the two-lane highway. Despite the traffic, Matisse chattered away about Climb Aloha, a store near St. Louis High School on the Leeward side of the island. The drawback in getting supplies from the place was twofold, as far as Arch was concerned. Some of the things they'd have to have for the climb would not be available in any shop on Oahu, period. And if they were, the prices would totally blow out the one credit card any of them had. But it was a moot point since the place, extolled as the greatest climbing store in the world by Matisse, wasn't open until one in the afternoon of the following day. The climb would have to be started long before that hour or they might be trapped on the side of the mountain for the night. Matisse appeared to be a bit out of shape and Arch had his damaged hand. There was only one place they were likely to get what they needed.

"Where we spend the night?" Matisse asked, his voice easily carrying over the convertible's wind noise since the car was moving at only about thirty miles per hour at most.

Arch didn't respond to Matisse's question because he didn't have an answer. As the old battered crate of an automobile burbled along with the traffic, Arch sat in the passenger seat of the Pontiac while the sun beat down through the spaces between the overhanging trees. He had no place to stay, without using even more credit that his card probably wouldn't bear. He really had no place to go back to. He had his agency retirement pay, but that barely equaled what he spent. Upon bitter reflection Arch realized the trip to Oahu, which he had booked as a round trip, was really a one-way trip. He was backed into a corner of his own making. He'd been there until the end of Vietnam, but had come home in physical and mental pieces, although he knew he would never, in reality, truly come home. He'd been through more trauma with the CIA, despite mission after mission being successful. He'd retired, but never truly come home from them, or the stuff he'd done with them, either. He had Virginia, the love of his life, Matisse, his only friend, and a Bellows mission of his own undertaking. He was determined to fight for her, keep Matisse as a friend, and figure out the riddle of the mission.

Matisse took a right when they finally inched up to, and through, the traffic light at Pupukea near Sunset Beach. He drove the smoking Bonneville all the way through the Foodland parking lot, and parked in one of the empty handicapped spots near the radar doors.

"We get some Poke to help us think," Matisse said, with one of his usual grins. He eased his wide and powerful frame from the Pontiac and slammed the door, as if to draw the most attention he could. "If they want move the car, show em your hand," he laughed. And walked away, leaving Arch frowning, wondering how a bandaged hand was supposed to qualify for handicapped parking privileges, but he said nothing.

"Stairway has changed," Ahi intoned quietly from the back seat. "Before you go there you must go see. They have guards at the bottom but not further up. You can get further up if you go Haiku way, and not easy way."

Arch turned, slinging his left arm over the broad back of the old car's bench front seat. "Why make two trips," he asked?

"Go to guards, and see what they can see further up. Stairway is not like some think. It's not ladder rungs drilled into the stone. It's mostly rusted and decayed actual steps, except in the steepest places. The stairway rolls over three hills before going up the highest point. There's two areas cleared at the top of hills. They call them platforms, but they're not really. They're just stops for the old cable car. Across the He'eia Stream Valley a huge cable is strung that goes up to the peak."

"Cable car?" Arch responded in surprise. "There's a cable car? And how do we get there through Haiku, the whole community's gated. They're not going to let us through."

"You don't go through Haiku Plantation," Ahi answered. That's wealthy homes and somebody would report you, anyway. You go to Waiaole Reserve and then cross first valley. At the top there you'll see the big freeway, H3, and you can see the end of the other road there. That's as far as I've ever been. From Hololio in Haiku all the way up the stream is an old Hawaiian burial ground. The warriors who were pushed over the Pali are there. Hawaiians don't go there ever."

"Oh great, a native burial ground," Arch said, exhaling deeply. "What about Matisse." He's Hawaiian. I can't go without him because of my hand."

"Matisse is Matisse. He doesn't believe in anything. He only makes believe because he thinks it makes me feel better. He's only Hawaiian by blood. It's why most locals don't want him around too much. He's like you that way. He doesn't really believe in anything or anybody, so nobody believes in him. He plays good ukulele and sings though."

Arch stared into Ahi's deep dark eyes but saw no humor whatsoever.

He turned back to see Matisse returning through Foodland's front door.

Arch couldn't play the ukulele and also couldn't sing worth a damn. He wondered if Ahi had intended to reduce him to almost nothing. Knowing that he had probably not meant anything personal, hurt even more.

Matisse climbed in, slammed the car door and shared the raw seasoned Poke around. Arch took a few chunks in his bare hands, only realizing how hungry he was when he consumed the first square cut chunk. Hawaiian Poke was the only raw fish he ever ate.

"Where we go? Take Ahi back, but where do we stay? My place not so good in Kalihi. Too many locals making trouble, and you too Haole. I got this under the counter. Only for locals like me."

"What's too local mean?" Arch asked, absently, but then realized it really didn't matter and he wouldn't understand whatever answer Matisse gave him anyway. "After Ahi, we go get the Lincoln. Then we take it to Kaneohe and get some gear. We have to hike in before sunset so we can reconnoiter the area at the base of the stairs."

"Reconnoiter. I like that word, and we going right to where the general lives? I like that too. We bare the bear in his den." Matisse replied, eating the raw fish one piece after another. The two pounds of "local special" Poke was gone in less than a minute. "Where we sleep tonight, out in the forest?"

"We'll see," Arch answered, evasively. "And it's 'beard the lion in his den.'"

"You think Haole woman stay with general?" Ahi asked, wiping his fingers on some of the many napkins Matisse had returned with.

Arch returned his gaze to the big Hawaiian in the back seat. "Maybe. I don't know. Maybe we just stay there."

For some reason Ahi thought the idea humorous. He laughed out loud with Matisse joining in. "We bare the lion," Matisse said, between laughs.

Matisse drove the Pontiac past Sunset to near the windmills of Kaaava where Ahi lived. The small, nondescript bungalow was set into a heavy stand of bamboo, and overgrown cane bushes.

"I give you my blessing," Ahi told them, as Matisse backed the Pontiac down the pulverized coral driveway, "I wish I could do more but I must take care of my people."

Neither Matisse nor Arch said anything until they were back in front of Virginia's house at Sunset. The black Lincoln sat where they'd left it earlier.

"You going to check it for bugs?" Matisse asked Arch, as Arch hit the fob button to unlock it.

"No. We really don't care. We just won't talk about anything until we're done at the base, and dump it back here. We'll never get into Kaneohe in your car."

"We really going to take over her house?" Matisse asked, climbing into the passenger side. "What if she comes back? What if Kurt and Lorrie show up armed to the teeth?"

"So what?" Arch answered. "We'll be ready for anything by then. We won't get back until after dark anyway. If anybody's there then we'll sleep in the car at the beach. I'm a little tired of being attacked by those people."

The drive to the base was silent and uneventful, although long because of all the North Shore visitors returning to Honolulu late in the day. Arch drove up to the Marine gate, showed his identification card and was immediately saluted. The guard passed the car through without comment, as Arch expected. The Bellows mission wasn't being shared with gate security.

The secret nature of whatever was going on made the whole project less secure for anybody who understood how such things work in the real world.

"There's a climbing store on the base?" Matisse asked Arch, in wonder.

"Regimental Supply," Arch told him. "There's a recon detachment working out of the base, and they'll have everything we need and more. It's Sunday so regular staff will be off. Hopefully we can convince whoever's left to let us make off with what we need."

Arch had to stop four different times to grill pedestrians about where the recon supply might be located. It turned out to be an old Quonset hut located next to the airstrip's main hangar. Arch drove right past all the signs warning against automobiles crossing the flight line. There was no activity in, or around, the huge closed hangar, and only one Humvee parked near the Quonset hut. He parked the big Lincoln next to the military vehicle, motioned for Matisse to wait, and walked through the unlocked hut door into the darkened interior. A small office window barely illuminated the domed structure's interior. Arch opened the office door without knocking but not before taking out his I.D. card. A staff sergeant sat looking at a computer monitor with his back turned.

"Staff Sergeant," Arch said his voice flat and hard.

The staff sergeant almost jumped from his seat, but still had the time to hit the kill switch for the monitor, as he flipped around preparing to salute. When he saw Arch's civilian attire he visibly relaxed but still remained at a position of attention.

"Sir," he responded, staring straight ahead and not at Arch.

"We need some gear sergeant," Arch indicated amiably, holding his card out over the narrow low counter.

The staff sergeant looked at the card briefly without taking it from Arch's hand. "Sir," he said with more emphasis, snapping back to attention.

"I need some climbing gear, the right binos, a set of NVGs and whatever else I can find, and I need it now. I've got a local doing the back work out in my Lincoln. See what you can do to help him." Arch walked out of the office without waiting to see what the staff sergeant's reaction would be. The number of general officers a sergeant in the Marine Corps might ever encounter personally, even during an entire career, was next to none and he was counting on the shock power of his rank, real or not.

The lights came on inside the hut and Arch went to work. It took almost fifteen minutes to find the necessary ropes, carbiners, gloves and anything else he felt they might need for the climb. He watched the sergeant almost balk when he pulled out a black box containing a brand new set of fourth generation night vision goggles. Losing a set of those could be career changing for any supply NCO, no matter what credentials the requesting officer had. But the sergeant carried them out, along with a couple of very expensive Leica binoculars.

"What do I put down for the use?" the sergeant asked, writing furiously near the back of the Lincoln while Matisse loaded everything into the trunk.

"Just put it down to the Bellows operation and I'll sign for everything," Arch answered, offhandedly. "We gotta move out before the sun goes down."

The sergeant looked up from his clipboard. "You're with General DeWare on Torch?" he inquired.

"You got it staff sergeant. Make it so," Arch used the words of Captain Piccard from *Star Trek: The Next Generation*, with a suppressed smile. He signed the clipboard, and then added his officer's serial number more for the sergeant's protection than his own.

Matisse's only comment before they got back inside the Lincoln caused Arch to smile. "This better store than Climb Aloha."

The trip back to Virginia's house was much faster than the trip to the base, as the traffic was all heading the other way. Once again, neither man spoke during the journey, in case the Lincoln really was bugged. There was nobody at the house, so they merely loaded everything from the Lincoln into the battered and damaged trunk of the Pontiac, before heading toward the forest preserve described earlier by Ahi.

It took only about half an hour to make their way back to the Japanese cemetery adjacent to Haiku Plantation. The road around the cemetery was unpaved, old, and overgrown by all manner of local flora. The Lincoln's paint job would have been ruined by their passage into the preserve. The Pontiac, however, once they arrived at the end of the road, seemed the same as it had been before they left. Arch looked at the car briefly, meeting Matisse's proud eyes, before helping him pull out the binoculars.

"We won't need the other stuff until tomorrow.

They had a rough idea of where they were going, because the huge elevated freeway was always visible in the distance. The two men trudged around the many trees and through the heavy bracken. There were multiple paths leading in all directions, but enough going the way they wanted to make the hike fairly easy. The small valley that preceded the larger valley with the stream at the bottom, proved almost effortless to negotiate. When they reached the top of the second rise, the freeway ran almost directly over their heads.

It was so high up, and set so deeply into the mountain-side, they could barely hear the trucks and cars passing above them. They settled into the top of the rise behind some fallen tree trunks and took out the binoculars.

"What do you see?" Arch asked, his face glued to the eyepieces of the Leica's.

"Right there," Matisse pointed.

Arch pulled back from his glasses to follow Matisse's pointing finger. He went back to the binoculars and found the object of Matisse's interest.

It was a chain link fence. He moved the sliding lever at the center of the binoculars to allow fifteen-power magnification. A white sign was hung on the inside of the chain fence. The large black letters of the sign warned: "Keep out. Government property. You are in danger of losing your life if you pass beyond this point without authorization." It was the same signs Arch had seen at Bellows, and many years before at the Los Alamos Laboratories in the high mountains of New Mexico. It was the definitive sign U.S. governmental forces used when they weren't kidding around.

"Watch," Matisse whispered, as if there was anyone closer than half a mile from their position.

Arch stared through the Leica lenses until his eyes hurt, and finally saw what Matisse was referring to. Once he pinned down a faint movement, and difference in coloration, he realized what he was looking at. Two roughly man-shaped figures stood behind the heavy vegetation near the fence. The fence had a large gate with railings just beyond the entrance. The gate was held shut by a large padlock holding thick, heavy chains together. The two men moved slowly back and forth, as if pacing across a very tiny parade ground. "Why they move?" Matisse asked.

"The enemy of all security," Arch replied. "Boredom. They never see anything. They're bored out of their minds. Probably don't even have cell phones so they won't be distracted. They aren't Marines though. Marines don't wear blue utilities. That would be Air Force or private security. Private security isn't likely but then neither is Air Force participation. Why would every damned service in the U.S. inventory be involved in this? It makes no sense at all."

"How we get around?" Matisse inquired; still staring through his own set of Leica's.

"See what they can see from where they are?" Arch asked back.

"They can't see dick! They can't even see us. The hill goes right up behind them," Matisse answered, gleefully.

"Exactly! That's what Ahi wanted us to see," Arch said, slowly bringing his glasses down to rest on top of one of the moist rotten logs they were resting on. "We'll come in from here tomorrow, and head right down into the valley before going up and around where the first platform must be. Then we go up."

XV

Matisse drove the Pontiac at breakneck speed. The traffic moving away from Haiku, back on Kam Highway, was spotty and moving faster than the speed limit, as well.

"I don't think it's a good idea to stay at that house," Matisse said, almost losing control of the swerving car in the middle of a sharp curve.

Arch watched a flock of wild chickens scatter, as the Bonneville came out of the curve, flattening out on it's rocky old suspension, and seemingly making for the birds at ever increasing speed. Arch knew Matisse was right. The house was a bad idea. But running all the way over the Koolau Mountains just to stay in the rotten, clap board, shithole Matisse lived in, was too awful to consider. And despite the bond they had formed, by accepting Virginia's bribe, Ahi had taken his offer of a place to sleep off the table.

"If she comes back, we'll just sleep in the Lincoln," Arch said loudly He had to raise his voice to be heard over the vortex of wind created by the convertible's racing along a straight stretch of highway. As they flew by, Arch noted Crawford's rest home, the two ancient concrete outbuildings falling, but still erect against the backdrop of the mountains.

"Why can't we just get a room at the Turtle Bay Resort?" Matisse complained, as the rich flora of the resort's grounds and golf course appeared just beyond the many ponds of Oahu's only shrimp farm.

"I don't know what's left on the card, and we may need gas or whatever before this is done," Arch replied. For the first time since leaving the service he wished that he was a team leader again, with a phony company's cash budget of mission money, and an unlimited American Express card. Being retired, before he'd come back to Oahu, had begun to feel an awful lot like being poor while waiting to die.

The house was as they left it. The Lincoln was still parked on the access road, apparently undisturbed by whatever electronics the Agency had, or had not, put in it. Both men walked back toward Sunset Beach; winnowed their way through small groups of tourists who had collected to watch the famous sunset; and then approached the house from the back. As soon as they climbed over the huge berm of sand, built up to protect against the giant surf of winter, they saw that the glass double doors of the house still gaped open.

Arch drained a bottle of Pabst Blue Ribbon he found in the fridge, ate half a bag of Maui potato chips in seconds, and then collapsed on the convertible couch without opening it. He heard Matisse rummaging around, grousing about how their presence in the house was a big mistake, until he fell into a deep sleep. His last thoughts were about his injured hand. It no longer hurt, but how could he climb anything with its' impaired capacity for grasping or holding.

A dream about Virginia shattered into tiny pieces as he was jerked awake. In a dream Arch left Virginia having breakfast at Pasqual's on Don Gaspar in Santa Fe, only to awaken to Virginia six inches in front of his face.

"What?" Arch exclaimed, instinctively moving his shoulder out from under her intrusive right hand.

"What are you doing in my home?" She hissed at him, while stepping back a few paces.

"I told you," Matisse informed Arch from the bottom of the stairs. "There's nothing about the Haole that's not bad news."

"Get out!" Virginia stated, her voice scathing, one finger of her hand extended and pointing toward the garage exit.

Arch sat up groggy, still trying to come back from the wonderful breakfast he'd just left behind. He could almost taste the bite of green chili in his mouth, instead of the bite in Virginia's tone.

"I thought you'd be with him," Arch forced out, shaking his head to clear it. "We didn't have any place on this side of the island to stay."

"Oh," Virginia replied, lowering her arm. She stared at him with an unbelieving expression on her face. She continued, "you didn't seem to have any problem remembering he's married before."

It was Arch's turn to say "oh."

"Let's go, we done here," Matisse said, moving toward the garage door. "There will be no sleep in this place, not as long as this Haole Elvira is here."

Virginia turned back to face him. "Island scum," she hissed out.

"Haole bitch," Matisse said right back.

"Alright, alright, are you two done? Arch asked. "This isn't a school bus. It's your place. We'll go. We're just been trying to help." Arch stood up before turning back to smooth out the couch, pick up the empty beer bottle, and half empty chip bag.

"Help?" Virginia said, her tone one of shock. " Help in your usual fashion. You just cost the Agency millions, and the Marine Corps a good chunk of its land. And it only took you a few days to accomplish that. Your usual help."

"Seems somebody here is owed something, by just about everyone who's taken over, including the U.S.

Government and the United States Marine Corps." Arch headed for the garage door with Matisse leading the way.

"I'll be here tomorrow morning if you want to come back and see me," Virginia said behind them, her tone softened, her words spoken low and slow.

Arch paused but did not stop. He gently closed the door behind him, not turning to look back. Back at the car, Matisse waited as Arch went through his pocket for the key fob.

"That's one screwed up Haole chick," he murmured, leaning over the cooling top of the black car.

"Oh shut it," Arch replied disgustedly, getting into the Lincoln, starting it and turning the air conditioning fan knob to its highest setting. "Screw it," he continued, "we're not sleeping in this God forsaken car. The Turtle Bay has got to have one room left, and I know they've got a computer in the business center. I'll transfer some money, if I have any money, into my credit car account. There's no way we can do what we've got to do tomorrow, without any sleep or having to use an outdoor shower."

Arch headed the Lincoln toward the Turtle Bay Resort, only realizing after a few miles that he was driving just like Matisse. He slowed the big cruiser until he came up upon a roadside fruit stand that always made him think of the great local tune called Sweet Old Lady of Waihole. He pulled coloration of its yellow spot, from where it'd lain ripening. Matisse picked up a couple of iced coconuts with the tops cut off. Back in the car he sucked noisily on his straw, holding the other one out to Arch, who was behind the wheel.

Both men exited the car under the portico at the resort entrance, sucking on their coconuts, and heading for the open-air check in counter. One of the bellmen asked Matisse if he or his partner had any luggage, causing the big Hawaiian to spill some of his coconut juice.

"We not Mahoos!" he yelled behind him with a twisted laugh.

"What's a Mahoo?" Arch asked, absently, bellying up to the counter where another aging Hawaiian worked with an outmoded cash register that had an Apple monitor somehow attached to it.

"You just get mad. I think you have bad temper, but you don't show it much," Matisse answered, setting his coconut next to Arch's on the counter.

The older Hawaiian finished working on the register, reached over, grabbed the coconuts, and tossed them into a trash basket.

Matisse glowered, while Arch took in a deep breath before speaking.

"We need a room. One room, two beds. We're not Mahoos," he informed the an older Hawaiian woman who was smiling in a seemingly friendly way, that didn't come across as friendly at all.

"That's good to know," the woman replied, "I wouldn't have guessed."

"The room, Kalani?" Arch asked, reading the woman's nametag and ignoring her snide comment.

"Name's not Kalani, just using her uniform, and yes, we have a room. Credit card and photo I.D.", she finished, holding out her left hand.

"How fitting," Arch said, reaching for his wallet. If the credit card didn't work, they'd be back to sleeping in the Lincoln.

Thankfully the card went through successfully. The woman wearing Kalani's uniform handed his stuff back, along with a small envelope with one plastic room key in it.

"Two keys," Arch instructed, trying to keep his voice civil.

The room was way out on the end of the ocean wing of the resort. It faced away from the ocean, but gave a wonderful view of the Koolau Mountains. Their lower swales peppered back to Kuhuku with giant windmills being turned slowly by invisible, and unfelt, wind currents. They went down to the lobby, after cleaning up as best they could without a change of clothes. In the morning they could get into the black climbing outfits Arch had conned from the Marine supply sergeant. He was able to transfer five thousand dollars to the credit card by completely draining his retirement account. When the first of the following month came, no bills would be paid unless his fortune changed.

They went from the business center, down to the outdoor bar near the pool. Matisse ordered two beers. Arch asked for a cup of coffee before remembering that the bar at the Turtle Bay didn't serve coffee. As he rose from his stool, Arch asked, "Why did you order two beers? You can't drink two at once?"

"Case I run out of money," Matisse answered, draining half of one of the bottles.

"But you don't have any money," Arch remarked, walking toward the pool. He headed toward some elevators where he'd seen employees, through an unmarked door in the hallway. He went through the door and ended up in a cafeteria. Employees were all over the place sitting at tables and talking. Nobody took notice of him standing there. Seeing a coffee machine he walked over, took a cup and poured. A woman behind the counter watched him, and then pointed toward a small refrigerator when he looked up at her questioningly. After adding half-and-half and a Splenda, he went back to the bar with his cup of coffee to rejoin Matisse, who still had the two bottles in front of him.

"At least you're not drinking too much," Arch said, taking his old seat. He looked at the tab before frowning. The tab had four beers credited to it.

"Thanks boss," Matisse responded with a big smile. An achingly beautiful sunset finished delivering its lingering effects, and they decided to call it a night.

Arch needed no alarm to awaken early the next morning. He roused Matisse. They cleaned up as best they could, the resort having supplied toothbrushes and small tubes of paste without room service needing to called. Arch called down to the front desk to have the car brought around, and then went down and punched his information into the ATM near the lobby restrooms. He took out a hundred, leaving less than that in his account. "Kalani" wasn't on duty so he had the front desk attendant make change. He wouldn't have minded giving the carhop a twenty, but old habits die hard. Too big a tip, or none at all, would be remembered. A medium tip would always allow the tipper to slip under unintended surveillance.

"Where we change?" Matisse asked, getting into the passenger side of the car.

"Shark's cove. There's a public restroom, and nobody will notice our black rubber outfits with all the SCUBA divers that hang around there.

It took ten minutes to reach Shark's Cove. Then another ten minutes to get changed and organize their gear before driving out on the Kam Highway to get to the Haiku area.

"We like Navy Seals," Matisse said. "We look too cool," he went on, tilting the rear view mirror to better see himself.

"I've never seen a three hundred pound Seal," Arch replied, dryly. He drove the speed limit, thinking about the complete idiocy of the quest they were on. They were totally unequipped to deal with any trouble, whatsoever. They had no communications equipment, nor anyone they could communicate with if they needed to. And they had no idea what they were looking for, what they would find, or if they'd find anything at all. On top of that, Arch himself was too old, and Matisse was too fat. Any talk of conditioning would only end in humor, if such talk ever occurred.

Arch was only clear about one thing, though, both he and Matisse were committed to a cause. Being committed to a cause, any cause, was better than not having one at all.

Sleeping in the car at Sunset

Visions. The green ghosts, the warriors and the Army officer of WWII

The hike in

The climb and the gear

The revelation

The descent back down into the valley

XVI

Arch scrapped the idea of hiking in through the Waialua Forest. The topography was just too difficult. By the time he and Matisse were anywhere near the base of the stairs, mid-day would long have passed. Heeia Stream ran all the way from deep inside the Koolau valley and only broke through to the surface near the base of Heeia Pier. Arch and Matisse sat just outside the Heeia Pier store. Old man Chow's kid, a man nobody could ever remember the name of, ran the place. The kid ran the place Hong Kong style. You could get anything you wanted at his store, if you had enough money and time. But the marine fuel concession he held really paid for the availability of the rest. Marine fuel was almost twice the price of regular gas, but in Hawaii any boat had to be run on it, instead of by the same gasoline put into cans at regular gas stations. The fact that half the price went directly into the concessionaire's pocket was never discussed. Boater's were used to the outrageousness of the arrangement, and the injustice at least meant that little places like Chow's small dive were dotted around the shoreline of Oahu.

There was a continuous stream of all kinds of people entering and leaving chows. When it broke up a bit, Arch asked Matisse "Tell me what you know about the climb." When Matisse didn't reply, he followed up with "Can we do it?" Matisse continued to consume his spam and eggs served over a hot sticky mass of white rice, turned black by a liberal pouring of Aloha Soy Sauce.

"Not climb," Matisse replied between bites, taking a swig of his four-dollar cup of Kona coffee. "Never climbed. But I heard from my brah," Matisse continued, "No ladders, no rungs, just metal steps with railings if they're still there. The whole thing is falling down, but ropes and equipment aren't important, or at least that's what my brahs used to say. Nobody talks about it anymore. I don't know why." Matisse went back to finishing up every last scrap of his breakfast.

Arch looked down at his injured hand with a sense of hope. He hadn't been at all certain that he would be able to do the climbing. He looked up and out over the bay. From where Arch sat he could see Kaneohe Marine Base clearly. His eyes were drawn to a small island sitting half way between the base and the end of the pier. Arch was one of the few residents of Oahu who'd ever visited the island. Coconut Island. The island that would have become famous if the producers of the old television show Gilligan's Island had continued filming there instead of only shooting the first three shows there. After those first episodes the show had bailed out and moved to a set in Los Angeles. Years earlier Arch used anthropology credentials to get out to the island, and had walked through the falling down sets still strewn about with fake rocks, and phony palm trees. The Department of Natural Resources denied all visits to regular citizens. Today nothing was likely left of the old Hollywood sets, as the University of Hawaii had taken it over to build a marine studies institute.

"Where we leave car?" Matisse asked.

"Isn't the community college right down from H3 there?" Arch replied, still staring at the island offshore.

"Yeah, but the parking lot for the mental hospital is even closer. Nobody will notice us," Matisse said.

Arch looked over at his companion to see if he was smiling, but Matisse seemed unaware of the humor buried inside his comment.

"How far to the stairs?" he asked, once again examining his hand.

"Not far. The Kapunahala stream has a path right to it under the freeway, but we have to climb a little hill to get up to it.

"I thought you said you've never been there," Arch responded in surprise.

"Nah, but my friends all have and they tell me. Kapunahala gets you in from one of the trolley platforms, and past the guards at the bottom."

"Let's go," Arch replied with a slight groan. He was not looking forward to what lay before them.

Arch had parked the car with its trunk facing the outside of the pier so they could get at its contents without anyone noticing. They worked in silence, packing ropes, pitons, bottled water and some spam and pressed rice musubi chunks that Chow sold for a buck a piece.

"You really think we need these?" Matisse asked, holding up a set of the brand new and frightfully expensive night vision goggles.

"Just put it in. I don't know. We may need all of this stuff or none of it. We won't be coming back down for supplies. That I do know. You said trollies, what trollies?"

"They had to carry all the stuff up there during the big war. They built concrete platforms on the lower peaks, and then strung trolley cables to the top."

"They still there?" Arch asked, standing up straight to adjust the straps of his backpack.

"Nah, they rusted away, but we can rest at the platforms on the way up," Matisse offered.

They drove to Windward Community College and then took the access road that ran along a tree line to the left. There was no gate separating the college campus from the hospital grounds behind it. Matisse drove the car past the last big building where there was a small parking lot not far from the wide stream. He parked the Lincoln in the only available slot. It had a small sign indicating why it was vacant.

"Police and fire vehicles only," Arch read, shaking his head in disgust.

"You a general," Matisse explained, getting out of the car.

"I'm not a real general," Arch replied, getting out of his side, knowing that the conversation was pointless, but continuing it anyway. "Even if I was a real general that wouldn't mean I could park where it says police and fire only."

"Almost same," Matisse replied, as expected, while putting on his backpack. He tossed the car keys to Arch after hitting the locking button, and making the Lincoln chirp and briefly blink its lights.

"They'll probably tow us," Arch said, despondently, staring back at the car and punching the button once again just to be sure.

"It's a rental," Matisse shot back over his shoulder, as if that explained everything.

The hike in took almost an hour. The overgrown path was the easy part, except where it crossed the flowing stream. The rocks under the water were covered with some slippery slime or lichen. Matisse's bare feet fared better than Arch's Teva sandals. He only fell once on the hike to the bottom of the "small" hill that was the base of the first platform.

"Little hill?" Arch said, staring up at the steep, flora-covered mess in front of him.

"No problem," Matisse answered with a laugh. He went right at the hill, until he was climbing upward on his hands and knees. "Mud good, it give us cover."

"Yes," Arch responded derisively, "we cover flat black with shiny brown mud. That'll work for us." Arch dug in behind Matisse, following him slowly up the incline. By grasping the deep-rooted tea leaf plants at the base, and then using them as handholds, they could move rather quickly by pulling hard to slide up through the red mud.

They reached the platform, after another hour of hard work. The concrete pad was covered with dried red mud. Arch rubbed some of the awful cloying stuff off on a nearby stanchion, realizing why the platform was so muddy. A lot of other people over the years had done the exact same thing. The base of the old trolley system was still there, but rusted away. The stairs coming up to, and then departing from, the platform were a surprise. They looked like regular basement stairs that might be found in a home, except they were fashioned from aluminum. Guardrails ran waist high on both sides of the stairs. Arch saw one immediate potential problem. The same slime and lichen that lined the rocks of the stream were all over the stairs. Both men dropped their packs. Matisse took out a bottle of water from his pack, and Arch grabbed his Leica binoculars. Arch studied the next platform, which was plainly visible by following the silver line of the stairs up to the next peak. Suddenly he saw rifle fire.

"Down," he yelled at Matisse, ducking behind a small concrete wall himself. There was no sound of a passing bullet, only the distant hollow boom of the rifle going off in the distance.

Matisse still stood as before, looking over at Arch and then toward the other platform. "What was that?" he asked, squinting his eyes.

Arch jumped up, swept across the few feet of mud coated concrete and pulled the big man to the deck.

"That was a rifle shot, you idiot," Arch breathed into Matisse's left ear, shoving away at his side until they were both behind the protection provided by the low, but thick wall.

"Somebody's shooting at us?" Matisse exclaimed, trying to raise his head to see what was going on. "Why? Who? Did you bring a gun? I didn't bring a gun."

"This isn't some sort of shoot 'em up mission. No, I didn't bring a gun," Arch replied angrily.

"It is now," Matisse answered, in a much softer tone. "What do we do? Do we climb back down and get outta here?"

Arch thought for a moment. "No," he said. "It's those two idiots again. And what they're doing tells us a lot. The other platform is about three hundred yards away. He could have hit me with any kind of decent rifle, but he didn't. Somebody predicted we'd make this attempt, and they want to deny access. Also, the fact that it's Kurt and Lorrie again tells us something. This whole thing's so secret, they can't have the Marines knowing anything. Because the Marines won't shoot at American citizens on American territory without a damned good reason."

"So what do we do?" Matisse asked.

Arch got to his feet, brushing away as much of the dry mud as he could, from his neat black outfit that was no longer neat or black. "We're going to proceed up the steps as if those clowns don't exist. They can shoot at us, but they can't shoot us. Arch walked over to where the steps connecting the platforms began. Two more shots echoed through the canyon. But Arch merely laughed gently, taking Matisse by one hand to pull him up like he was a fallen child. "Come on, this was my business. I know these people. I know this game."

Matisse slowly got to his feet, his hands visibly shaking. "What if they miss?" he asked, peering with unaided vision at the other platform.

"What do you mean? They are missing," Arch said, ignoring the other platform and getting his pack readjusted to his back.

"I mean, they are missing on purpose, but what if they miss a miss?"

As Matisse kept talking he too began getting ready for their next leg of the climb.

"We may need a gun though, so I hope those two are around when we get up there," Arch said, steering Matisse toward the first step.

"Why would we want that?" Matisse answered, taking both railings in his big meaty hands. .

"Because they're idiots. We'll take their guns."

Matisse stood with his hands on the rails, unmoving. "I'm not sure about all this. They're shooting at us, these steps don't look safe, and I don't know what's up there."

"Stop worrying. Most of the things you worry about in life never happen. And the things that do, happen in ways you could never have figured out ahead of time," Arch said, pushing gently against Matisse's broad back.

"Okay, but I don't know," Matisse answered. He then stepped forward, plunging ten feet down into a huge vat of red mud. The collapse of the aluminum stair, his downward slide, and even the impact of his body landing, was all nearly soundless. Only a rifle shot in the distance, playing over the top of the ceaseless trade winds, put an audible exclamation point on the event.

"Boss?" Matisse yelled up from the vat of mud, still stuck.

"Assholes," Arch murmured, looking over to the other platform.

"It's just another warning Matisse. I'm coming down to get you out."

Arch climbed down, but by the time he reached him, Matisse was already out of the hole. "We just have to continue," he told the Hawaiian, "and put up with their juvenile pranks."

"Yeah, okay boss. But you go first. And we need a gun just to feel better. Then we can miss on purpose too. Or not."

There were no more shots or weakened sections of stairs. It took another hour to reach the third platform. It was abandoned. Cigarette butts were scattered about, and Lorrie hadn't policed his brass. Arch found a brass cartridge casing with .243 stamped into its base. Arch remembered something that had slightly bothered him when he saw the rifle go off near where they'd been standing. It looked vaguely familiar. Now he was certain. The rifle was a Mannlicher-Schoenauer in .243. It was either the same rifle, or an exact replica, of the one he'd presented to Virginia on her fiftieth birthday. He knew, deep down in his heart, that he'd just been shot at by the same rifle he'd given the love of his life, less than a year earlier. He went numb.

"Where you go?" Matisse yelled in his ear, shaking him by one shoulder.

"What?" Arch answered, his voice flat and dead.

"Man, you were gone boss. You took a moment off there. Senior moment they call it. Maybe a stroke. You don't look so good. I don't think calling 911 will do much good. I don't think they'll come up here."

"I'm fine. Fucking "A" fine. What do you want?"

"Boss, you fine, but somebody going to die. I hope it's not me. It's her again, isn't it? Even all the way up here. Where do we go now?"

"The next platform," Arch murmured. "It's going to be dark before we get all the way to the top. It's good we brought the NVGs."

"And the spam. Chow's musubi is almost as good as his pork hash. But I don't like this night stuff. It's creepy and we got some bad buys who don't like us at all."

"I didn't know," Arch said, his voice sounded vague and far away, even to him.

"About the night? About our enemies?" Matisse inquired, rubbing his head and looking down at the already darkening valley below.

"About the pork hash," Arch answered. "I love pork hash but you can't find any good stuff anymore. Patty's Kitchen closed. Now there's a place in Minoa, but that's it. I love pork hash, and the night. It's going to be a good night."

"Boss, you're scaring me. What happened? Something happened? What we going to do?"

"Make camp," Arch said. "Start a small fire. I like my spam and rice warm. We'll climb at first light."

"A fire?" Matisse repeated, his voice rising. "Everyone will see us. We'll be sitting ducks, boss. Everyone will think we're fools."

"Fools?" Arch said, more to himself than Matisse. "Yes, they will. I've been a terrible fool. Tonight we'll have hot spam and rice with a bit of Aloha soya, and tomorrow morning early hell is coming to breakfast."

XVII

They climbed the steps to an area just below the third platform. The climb wasn't a challenge for either of them, but looking beyond that platform they could see that the final stretch would be more difficult. They climbed down to a small glade, covered with pine trees overhanging the distant valley below. Matisse gathered plenty of dry branches, old needles, and cones from the protected areas under the big pines. They huddled together and had a fire going in seconds.

"So tell me boss. What happened?" Matisse asked, and then waited.

A full minute went by, but Arch didn't respond.

"I'm here," Matisse complained softly. "I came with you. I'm out here. I got shot at too."

"The rifle," Arch started out, but then stopped for a few seconds. "The rifle Lorrie used to shoot at us was the same one I gave Virginia for her birthday last year." He finished and stared glumly into the fire.

"You gave the Haole bitch a rifle for her birthday?" Matisse asked.

Arch nodded, not looking up. "Don't call her that," he followed, his voice barely audible. "It's racist."

"Racist?" Matisse countered, in surprise, "because, I called her a Haole or a bitch?"

"Haole means white and it means white in a very negative way. We both know it, and I don't like it. Never have."

"So I can't call you a Haole anymore?" Matisse asked. "You use it like Marines use swearwords for their friends. It's a term of endearment, so I don't care."

"Okay, brah, then I won't call her that. I'll just call her Virginia the bitch."

Arch looked over at his friend, munching away on another block of musubi, and silently let out his breath in resignation.

"You gave the bitch rifle. We got shot at by same rifle." Matisse started to laugh.

"What?" Arch finally said, more to shut Matisse up than wanting an answer.

"It's funny," Matisse got out between quieting laughs.

"What's so funny?" Arch said. "Virginia loves guns,"

"You give gun to woman, and we get shot at by same gun. Logical in a, Haole way. No offense. Not good. What we going to do?" Matisse asked before going back to eating and poking the small fire with a stick.

"They know we're here. Hell, everyone knows we're here. Those rifle shots echoed around the entire windward side of the island. Almost nobody shoots anybody in Hawaii, unlike what's on television shows. The islands have the lowest level of violence in the whole country. Maybe two people shoot anyone on this side of the island in a year, and it's not with a high-powered rifle. So, the police will eventually be coming, but it doesn't matter. We're climbing tonight, once we're rested and fed."

"We're climbing at night?" Matisse said, his voice little more than a weak whisper. He stopped taking bites from the musubi, and stared across the fire at Arch.

"Night vision," Arch said, taking a few of the musubi from his own pack. "We can't climb up to the third platform because they'll stay waiting. We've got to climb around it. They won't expect us to try that at night. We'll leave everything here, including the food and water. When dawn breaks, we'll go up with only the binoculars, my Leica camera and some rope, to see what we can see beyond the platform breaks. This whole thing is coming down to what's hidden in one valley on this island. Everything else is directed toward that, or about that. I looked at all the Koolau peaks with the binoculars, and there's nothing up there except some old radio antennas. It's got to be the big valley just on the other side of the Koolau range. Nobody goes into that valley, because it's a protected part of the watershed drinking supply for Honolulu."

Arch rummaged through his pack for the NVGs, then used the firelight to located the on/off switch. He turned the set on, and brought the rig up to his eyes, without pulling the elastic straps around his head. He looked out across the valley. The valley appeared as if it was an overcast afternoon, rather than the near total darkness it was in. There was no color but at least the image was in black and white, not the green glow given off by earlier generations of the devices. He pushed one of the buttons on the left side of the rig. A changing number instantly appeared on the lower left side of the tiny screens he was looking at. Arch moved his head from side to side and the numbers changed. He realized that the glasses were giving him the range to some points across the valley. He pulled his head back and stared at the set. There was no laser light coming from it, which meant it was emitting infrared laser light to calculate the range. Which also meant it was very dangerous to handle. If either he or Matisse were to look directly into the invisible beam, it could easily cause blindness. He put the rig back on and pushed the side of the remaining 'rocker' button. The other side of the valley zoomed toward him. Magnification. Arch smiled to himself.

"Man, they've come a long way since the earlier days with these," he said to Matisse. He held out the rig and showed Matisse how to work the buttons.

"Can I sell these when we're done? If we don't get killed, I mean?"

Matisse said, playing with the features and holding up the goggles to his face.

"Let's get ready. Neither one of us is in the greatest shape for this and there's not much room on the steep slopes of that peak. The terrain is the real enemy, since Virginia has apparently instructed those two clowns not to shoot us," Arch said, unloading his pack by the fire. "We'll leave the fire burning. The hot embers will draw the attention of whatever they've got to spy on us with."

Matisse put the NVG's down and leaned forward. His large upper body slowly canted back and forth, gently.

"What are you doing?" Arch asked. "Get ready, it'll be full dark soon and the glasses work best when there's little light."

"Ho'oponopono chant, Hawaiian prayer," Matisse replied after almost a full minute. "It's to clear my thoughts, my soul, and to say I'm sorry." "Are you ready now?" Arch asked.

"For everything. I'm ready now." Matisse grabbed his own pack, and pulled a fifty-foot climbing rope out, along with his own glasses.

As both men worked to get ready for the climb, the wind blew steadily over their heads, and up toward the summit of the mountains above them.

"What's the vegetation like up ahead?" Arch asked.

"The red blossoms all around are from Ohia trees," Matisse responded, stopping to point with one hand up toward the blackening darkness of the ever-rising range of mountains. They grow low, and have all kinds of branches. We have to go around them because they're so thick. The bigger trees are Koa, but not many of them left. Further up, if we get there, are the Loulu palms. Shaped like fans, but bigger. The Ohia branches are small enough to hold on to."

When they were ready to climb, Arch checked his Brequet. "We should make it around the platform in a couple of hours. We'll circle back and hit the stairs. From there it should be a clear shot straight to the top. Probably more than a thousand steps, but even at night it shouldn't be a problem if we have enough time."

The going got difficult as soon as they were a few yards reaching it required penetrated the six inches or so to the hard lava rock below. Matisse's bare feet worked better than Arch's with his Teva sandals constantly being sucked from the bottom of his feet. The branches of the Ohia trees were not nearly as helpful as the roots of the many ferns, and other vegetation that was buried deep into the mud, and sometimes tied right into the rock surface below. They had to climb sideways to move around the conical peak. The third platform was on the top of the peak. Reaching it, however, required more grasping and sliding than climbing. They didn't stop for two hours, until Arch found a small, basically level clearing about the size of a king size mattress. Both men lay gasping for air, and much needed rest.

"My hand is killing me," Arch said, pulling his goggles off and setting them aside. His hand was too close to be seen with the goggles on, since they couldn't focus on anything less than five feet away. Matisse leaned forward with his Bic lighter

"They'll see us," Arch hissed, "put that thing out."

"What they going to do, brah, shoot and miss us some more?" Matisse laughed, extinguishing the flame.

"Thanks though," Arch squeezed out, trying to massage the mess that was his hand. The bandages had been indistinguishable from the mud covering them. Only the red of his blood seeping through had indicated anything about the wound. "I can't climb anymore. We've got to go up and get on the stairs. We've got to take our chances that we're far enough past the platform."

It took only a few minutes for both men to recover, and begin the climb. The going was steep, as they went straight up the mud and plant covered hill, digging in their feet and thrusting upward with their thighs. It was slow going. And, Arch could only feel his way along, rather than attempt to grasp branches, or plant roots for support. Matisse, clunking his head against metal, alerted them when they reached the stairs. The aluminum was intact, as only aluminum could have been over the years of lying unattended in such moisture rich conditions. Nobody seemed to take any notice of them as they climbed the last few feet and mounted the stairs.

"Slippery," Arch complained, almost falling on the first step he attempted.

"We're covered in mud and these are always wet anyway," Matisse joined in.

They used the railings to climb, almost more than the stairs themselves. Matisse counted off backwards, singing the words to "Ninety-Nine Bottle of Beer on the wall," until Arch couldn't take the sing song, repetitive, idiocy of the lyrics any longer.

"Will you shut it, they're going to hear us!" he almost yelled. The higher they'd climbed, the greater the winds velocity.

"Oh sure, they hear us," Matisse laughed from just behind him. "High wind, rain, mud and muck and we're so far above this crazy island that a plane's likely to hit us, and they gonna hear us. Sure boss." But he stopped singing.

It took a couple of hours for them to reach a place close to the top. The stairs, without warning, abruptly stopped well before reaching the edge of the peak. With their goggles, they stared back and forth along the inside of the top of the ridge. A very faint path ran along the edge about fifteen feet down from the very top. Along the path, as far as they could see, ran an almost four-inch-thick cable. It was brand new and colored to match the foliage. Arch squatted down to closely examine the cable, shifting around to look back in the direction they'd come from. Where was the cable from and where did it go?

"Kaneohe's all lit up," Matisse pointed out, looking in the same direction. The base seemed to have every light turned on, although there was no activity visible from such a great distance. Kam Highway was lit from place to place, as it meandered the length of the island before disappearing near Turtle Bay. Only the fact that the highway lights abruptly ended, marked where that location must be.

"They're down there," Matisse said, his goggles aimed down the stairs.

"Yeah," Arch agreed, seeing a glow of faint light emanating from the platform they'd so laboriously gone around.

"Which way?" Matisse asked.

Arch looked around. "Haleiwa way," he said, finally. There being no point in going in the other direction. The valley was between their position, and that of Pearl Harbor, which was more toward Haleiwa than Diamond Head. Without further discussion, they got up and moved to the narrow path. Arch led, holding his damaged hand against his stomach, and using his right arm for balance. They came to a point where the path began to rise. Looking up, they saw that the very top lip of the mountain range ran both ways about forty feet higher up. Arch stopped and crouched down again.

"We might as well climb up and wait," he said. Matisse didn't reply, simply continuing to wait behind him on the path.

Very slowly, and gingerly, Arch and Matisse worked their way up to the edge, again using the cable to push up from. The ridge ran, broken here and there by breaks, like the Pali cleft, which ran from Bellows Beach beyond Hawaii Kai, all the way across Oahu to finally expire just above the North Shore town of Haleiwa. Arch eased the Leica binoculars from one pocket, and his camera from the other. He breathed in and out a few times, without giving in to his desire to look back, or down, from where he sat wedged into the rocky, muddy bracken with Matisse. He set the camera lens to its maximum optical enlargement of twenty times, and then 'pushed' that out to forty using digital enlargement as well. The knob for those adjustments was located right next to the shutter button. What he might get from the beautiful German device without being able to read the settings properly he didn't know. All he could do was set the enlargement to max, and hope that putting the rest on automatic would capture something.

Arch dug both Tevas deep into the mud, and angled forward and up until his shoulders were level with the top of the sharp rock ridge. Matisse surged up beside him. Arch removed his night vision goggles carefully, knowing he'd probably never need them again. The distance down into the valley below was too great for the night vision device to return any image of distinguishable quality. Matisse had his pair of binoculars, but no camera. If there was anything to be permanently recorded, it was up to Arch's Leica.

He looked down through the lens of his binoculars, but it was too dark to see into the valley below. The sun was set to rise off of Honolulu, and the blackness of the sea there was distinguishable beyond the city's outline. It was easy to tell where Pearl Harbor was, but Diamond Head was barely recognizable only because Arch knew exactly where to look for it. Arch let his binoculars hang down from the safety cord around his neck. Matisse did the same.

"Too dark down there," Arch observed.

"Not for long, dawn's almost here," Matisse observed, scratching his head and then popping two spam musubis out of his shirt pocket. Breakfast boss?" he offered, holding one out in his right hand. "I'm really tired. Maybe there's nothing there. All of this for nuthin' except to be messed with by the bitch's goons."

Arch took the musubi and bit off a piece. He was too tired himself to argue. He shifted his position to favor his damaged hand, but slid part way back down the slope.

"Come on, let's tie ourselves to some of this shrubbery so we can rest a bit," he instructed Matisse, unlimbering the rope from around his neck after taking off his binoculars.

The securing job only took up a few feet of the thin but extremely strong climbing rope. Matisse tied the two ropes together, around them and then up and around the base of a low Ohia tree, located right near the very top edge of the mountain ridge.

"Special Hawaiian knot," Matisse said with satisfaction when he was done. "One pull on that loop and we are free." He dropped the remainder of the joined ropes down the cliff face beneath them. Arch watched the rope snake down until the bottom of it settled onto a steep decline, covered with a green carpet of taro plants and ferns.

Arch nodded off, letting the rope take his weight, but was awakened only seconds later, or so he thought at first, until he saw Matisse fully asleep next to him. It was barely light out. They'd slept right into early dawn.

"Matisse," he hissed as silently as he could, reaching around to poke the big thick Hawaiian in the neck with the index finger of his good hand.

Matisse jerked awake, and they both struggled to crawl the few feet back up to the lip, after Arch recovered his binoculars from the mud next to him, thankful that the Leica's hadn't fallen to the valley floor below.

Arch peered through the lenses down into the valley on the leeward side of the range. He took a quick scan and then pulled his glasses down to try to clean them. The lenses were clear. Bringing the Leica's back up to his eyes, he looked down into the valley again.

"Jesus Christ," he breathed out, and then said the words over and over again, staring into the distance.

"What is it?" Matisse asked, his own eyes glued to the scene below.

A silver object lay isolated inside a circle of heavy foliage in the valley below. Arch figured the object to be about a hundred feet long and about twenty in diameter, judging from the few pieces of heavy equipment working around it. Both ends of the object were rounded. It looked like a giant silver hot dog with raised circles protruding around both ends a few feet from the ends. The raised metal circles looked like giant rivets. The area around the object was cleared red dirt but the backhoes and caterpillars weren't clearing forest. It became obvious that they were burying the object as quickly as they could.

"Shit," Arch whispered, dropping the glasses to his chest and reaching for the camera. He touched the shutter button. The camera's lens extended out to its maximum and its back screen lit up. He hit the autofocus button and the object zoomed up at him. "Shit," he said again, this time without whispering.

"Brah, that's not right. Not right. There's something wrong," Matisse followed, his voice matter-of-fact, his inflection dead flat.

"God...good God...it's not real," Arch said, his own tone one of shock and disbelief.

The object was changing. The 'rivets' slowly faded and then re-appeared and then did it again. Arch moved the control for video in order to catch the changes.

"They blinking," Matisse whispered, "they blinking like lights but not lights. Here and not here. Man, this scaring me."

"I'm getting it on video—" Arch said, until the bullet hit and blew a large chip form the lip of the ridge between he and Matisse. The sound of the shot came seconds later from behind them. Arch cringed but managed to hit the off button on the camera and slide it into his pants pocket. A split second later Matisse, in a panic, pulled the Hawaiian loop he'd carefully tied into the climbing rope.

Arch fell, sliding down to hit the cable he'd seen located just above the path twenty feet below. He slid off the cable and onto the path itself, which instantly gave way. There was nothing to hold onto. For the half second he was seemingly stationary Arch's body rotated outward until he was looking out over the entire expanse of the leeward side of Oahu coming alive with the morning sun. The soft beauty of the scene was instantly replaced by total terror in Arch's mind. He plummeted downward facing out, his body having no contact at all with the cliff face as his speed increased. He heard Matisse scream from somewhere nearby but all he could do was watch the green carpet they'd viewed from above come up at him with tremendous speed.

Just before impact Arch felt a huge jerk at his waist, twisting him completely around, and then the pressure was gone. Arch hit the severely angled green carpet on his back and kept going. Head first his body plunged, wildly sliding down the face of the Koolau Mountains, his view only of the clouding blue sky above. His arms were pinned by the speed of his passage and his back felt like he was receiving the worst Korean massage of all time.

The slide seemed to take minutes but Arch knew it could only be taking a few seconds. Seconds before death. Then he was in the air again, this time tumbling until he impacted the water. He didn't know how he hit or where, all he could feel was pain all over so bad he couldn't move.

"Matisse," he squeaked out to the sky, lying on his back in the stream, his head somehow indented into the soft mud of one bank.

"I'm here. Oh, this is bad," Matisse responded from nearby.

"We're alive," was all Arch could get out in reply.

"We're back in the stream where we started, back in the valley," Matisse concluded.

Both men lay within yards of one another. Matisse had landed with his face in the bank. Arch rolled to all fours and looked over at him, and then started to laugh. Matisse began to laugh with him until they were shoulder to shoulder facing downstream. Tear runnels formed on both of Matisse's cheeks.

"I can't walk," Matisse said, "I can't make my body move."

Arch looked behind Matisse. "Your part of the rope is around a tree," he said, starting to laugh again.

They slowly untied themselves from the remnants of the climbing rope. Even without the rope they were too weak to get up and walk, so they crawled.

"Just like last time. We crawl in the streambed. Haole God has a sense of humor."

"Haole God. Racist!" Arch replied. "You prayed to Pele or whoever that Hawaiian God is. The forgiveness God, the God of love. How did that work for us?"

"We alive," Matisse concluded, his voice growing stronger as they crawled under the heavy growth, the coolness of the fresh water bringing life back into their abused bodies. "Nobody could live through that. Hawaiian warriors were thrown off of the Pali and they all died. Not one warrior lived. Pele was on Kamehameha's side. Now he on our side."

"I can't argue with your logic, but I think we aren't out of trouble yet. In fact, after what we saw we may be in deeper than ever." Arch agreed.

"What did we see?" Matisse asked, stopping to wash the mud from his face. "Better?" he asked, looking over.

"No. I like you in that browner shade," Arch answered.

"What we see?" Matisse asked again.

"I could say anything, because that's what we saw. Something different. Little green men come to mind. If it was something out of our own inventory they wouldn't be burying it like that." Arch stopped for a moment to consider after trying to answer Matisse's question. He pulled himself to a nearby tree of some species or phylum he couldn't identify, and slowly raised himself to a vertical position. I think I can walk. Your legs okay?"

"It's not my legs bad," Matisse complained, getting to his own feet. "It's my head. I no want what's in it. The bitch said we didn't want to know. She was right about that."

It took all morning for them to reach the area of the parking lot where they'd left the Lincoln. It was still there.

"Where we go?" Matisse asked, getting into the passenger side of the hot car.

Arch turned the air on full. "There's only one place to go. Now we know why the Marine base is a hive of activity. Nobody knows what's going on there except a few people but everyone knows there sure as hell is something happening. The big plane at Bellows? The nuclear reactor aboard, if that's what it is? The cable up on top? We don't know a whole lot except we know a whole lot too much. We're either in this thing or we're dead. I knew Virginia was in way over her head but I had no idea it was this deep. There's never been a 'this deep' before."

"The bitch's house?" Matisse asked.

"Where else," Arch answered, accelerating away from the school with his foot on the floorboard.

"More better!" Matisse exclaimed with a laugh.

When they arrived at the Sunset House Matisse noticed right away that the Pontiac was gone.

"They stole my car! They took my Bonneville. The best car on the island. My convertible."

"Will you shut up," Arch ordered. "We've got more serious stuff to consider than the heap of junk you call an automobile."

Two Suburbans were parked outside the gate but the gate and garage door were both closed. Arch pushed the buzzer but nobody answered.

"Assholes," he whispered to the inert box.

They walked all the way back to Sunset Beach and came to the rear of the house. The sliding glass doors were open and the drapes billowed out.

"See, just like before. We in time warp," Matisse noted, pointing.

"Stop with the science fiction crap," Arch said, forcefully. I don't believe in aliens. So, they might have been here before. So what? They're not flying around over our heads all the time watching us. I don't believe that."

"Not over our heads. Down in the valley," Matisse corrected.

"Shit," was all Arch could think to reply.

They walked through the double doors. Sitting around the great room table just inside was the whole collected group they'd been encountering since the beginning. Virginia sat on the couch next to the general. He was attired in light khaki uniform for the first time since Arch had met him. On the other couch Kurt and Lorrie sat, with Kurt cradling his arm similar to the way Arch held his own, but not oozing blood

Arch stopped at the shorter base of the coffee table when Frank, his former partner walked in from the kitchen.

"What's he doing here?" Arch asked of Virginia, glaring into her eyes.

Frank walked across the room and took a seat at one of the empty chairs at the end. He said nothing about Arch's remark or in his own defense, only murmuring, "Arch," as he took the seat.

Arch was about to explode when the drapes parted and Ahi came through the double doors and walked to his side.

"Gentlemen, if you would please sit down, we'll talk," the general said, his voice gentle but seeming to possess a core of iron.

Ahi and Arch took the last two seats.

"So who talks first, and about what?" Arch asked.

"You just did and that's two questions," the general answered. "The second question is the one were all here about."

Arch looked around the table and sized everyone up according to body language. He started and finished with Virginia. He'd lost her. He could see it in her movements next to the man she was obviously with in more ways than one. She moved as if she was a part of the man, even though they were separated by inches. The meaning of life was all Monty Python's and Arch could not get those movie images from his mind to the point where he almost laughed out loud.

"And so?" Arch asked, since nobody else said a word.

"We don't know, and we know you don't either," the general stated matter-of-factly. "You're in because you know. Your opinion and advice would be appreciated. It'd be appreciated from all of you," he said spreading his hands to encompass the whole group.

"Oh great, not just a few hours ago your people took a killing shot at us up on that mountain," Arch forced out, his anger and disappointment in Virginia coming through in his acidic tone.

"That was Kurt being personal," the general commanded. "Apologize to the man Kurt and tell him you're glad you missed. And you too Frank. You were under orders but what they hell, the man has a point. Everything's changed. This isn't about personal animosity, the Marine Corps, Hawaii or much of anything else other than the potential survival of the human race."

Arch let his shoulders slink down. There was just no point in demanding anything of anyone in the group or recriminations. The general had stated things the way they really were as clearly as possible.

"What about the cable running across the top of the Koolau range, and the huge plane and nuclear plant aboard it at Bellows?" Arch asked, not giving either Kurt or Frank the opportunity to mouth meaningless platitudes of apology.

"The plane's powering the radio interference antennas you couldn't see," the general responded, "he one's suppressing radio transmissions coming out of the object. The plane's carrying the nuclear power plant for that but also a nuclear weapon in case it's needed, since they don't store them at Pearl anymore and the Navy hasn't been brought into this yet."

"How can that be? A supposed alien craft transmitting regular old radio signals?' Arch asked, in surprise.

"We don't know but we do know there's nothing regular about anything dealing with the object," Virginia answered. "The White House wants total containment so we can't even get expert scientific opinions about much of anything yet. The White House doesn't know about any of you, either," she said, looking to Ahi and Matisse before coming back to meet Arch's gaze.

"What about my Bonneville?" Matisse asked.

"We towed it away for repairs on the base. It was the least we could do for you," the general said.

"Where do we go from here?" Arch asked into the silence.

Nobody said a word. The general looked over at Virginia who smiled at Arch with what he now considered a cold smile.

"Down into the valley, of course," she said.

The end of Book One.
Stay tuned for more Arch Patton adventures.
*Visit **www.JamesStraussAuthor.com**.*

James Strauss was born into a U.S. Coast Guard family during WWII. He's live in thirty-four places — from South Manitou Island in Michigan to Honolulu Hawaii — and held positions, with credentials, to serve in over twenty-five careers, ranging from University Professor in Anthropology, deep sea diver, and Physician's Assistant to U.S. Marine Corps Officer, police officer, and novelist.

Mr. Strauss enjoyed publishing three novels (*The Boy, The Warrior,* and *The Bering Sea*); written numerous television and movie screenplays; and currently publishes a weekly newspaper, *The Geneva Shore Report,* in Lake Geneva, Wisconsin, where he lives with his wife of forty-seven years.

Made in the USA
Columbia, SC
21 May 2017